Harlequin Romance® presents...

Jackie Braun

*Her believable characters and fresh voice
will pull you into the drama...and have you
turning the pages all night long!*

Don't miss book three of this exciting trilogy.

Coming next month:

**Dane's story in
Saying Yes to the Boss #3905**

D0036177

Books by Jackie Braun

HARLEQUIN ROMANCE®
3897—A WOMAN WORTH LOVING*

The Conlans of Trillium Island

Don't miss any of our special offers. Write to us at the
following address for information on our newest releases.

Harlequin Reader Service
U.S.: 3010 Walden Ave., P.O. Box 1325, Buffalo, NY 14269
Canadian: P.O. Box 609, Fort Erie, Ont. L2A 5X3

Dear Reader,

A woman's first love holds a very special place in her heart. All these years later, I can still remember what I was wearing when I received my first real kiss, as well as the maudlin songs I played over and over on the stereo when that boy dumped me for someone else.

Ali Conlan's childhood sweetheart broke her heart, too. First loves never last. Or do they? In exploring that question I came up with *Their Unfinished Business*.

As the title implies, Luke and Ali have not quite gotten over their past relationship. Of course, both of them like to think they have. Luke is now a successful businessman, but when he returns to Trillium Island as an investor in the Conlans' resort, he soon realizes that what he and Ali once shared is exactly what his life has been missing the past ten years. My headstrong heroine takes some convincing, though.

I hope you enjoy the second story of my CONLANS OF TRILLIUM ISLAND trilogy. Just wait till you find out what I have in store for Dane. His story, *Saying Yes to the Boss,* is coming from Harlequin Romance in August.

Best wishes,

Jackie Braun

THEIR UNFINISHED BUSINESS

Jackie Braun

The
Conlans
of Trillium
Island

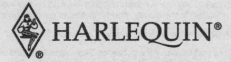

HARLEQUIN®

TORONTO • NEW YORK • LONDON
AMSTERDAM • PARIS • SYDNEY • HAMBURG
STOCKHOLM • ATHENS • TOKYO • MILAN • MADRID
PRAGUE • WARSAW • BUDAPEST • AUCKLAND

ISBN-13: 978-0-373-03901-2
ISBN-10:   0-373-03901-8

THEIR UNFINISHED BUSINESS

First North American Publication 2006.

Copyright © 2006 by Jackie Braun Fridline.

Jackie Braun earned a degree in journalism from Central Michigan University in 1987 and spent more than sixteen years working full-time at newspapers, including eleven years as an award-winning editorial writer, before quitting her day job to freelance and write fiction. She is a past RITA® Award finalist and a member of the Romance Writers of America. She lives in mid-Michigan with her husband and their young son. She can be reached through her Web site at www.jackiebraun.com

"I envy Ali Conlan her lake view. Okay, Trillium Island is fictional, but Lake Michigan is real. Anyone who has had the privilege of watching the sun sink into that vast Great Lake knows that no camera has yet been invented that can capture the pure magic."
—Jackie Braun on *Their Unfinished Business*

This one's for the girls:
Monica, Kelly and Teresa.
Enduring friendships are a rare gift.
Thank you.

PROLOGUE

"No. No way. Absolutely not!"

Ali Conlan crossed her arms over her chest and glared at her twin sister across the dinner table.

"What's the big deal?" Audra asked. Arching her brows, she added, "I mean, unless you're not over him. *Alice.*"

It turned out a person really could see red when mad, Ali realized as her vision tinted crimson.

Through gritted teeth, she said tightly, "Don't call me Alice. And I *am* over Luke Banning. I was over him five minutes after he left town *with you* eleven years ago."

If her sister wanted to fight dirty, she would fight dirty right back, Ali decided.

But Audra didn't so much as blink before replying blandly, "And you've forgiven me for leaving and for that little...misunderstanding. Why don't you give him the same break? It was a long time ago. You need to move on."

"I have moved on!" Ali hollered, tossing down her

napkin and rising slightly from her chair. She sounded defensive even to her own ears, but it didn't help that her one-time, two-bit actress of a sister said *sotto voce,* "Me thinks she doth protest too much."

Reeling in her temper, Ali glanced around the table where her brother, Dane, and Audra's husband, Seth Ridley, sat. Clearing her throat, she said more calmly, "I am over Luke Banning. I haven't spent the past eleven years pining for the man. In fact, I've hardly given him a second thought. I've been too busy."

"Oh, yeah? When was the last time you had a date?" Audra asked.

It felt good to be able to say, "I have one this weekend, as a matter of fact. With Bradley Townsend."

"The developer?" Dane made a face.

"Actually, he's a man," she drawled.

"I'm not sure I like him," her brother said. Audra, amazingly, did not offer an opinion. In fact, she had become suddenly engrossed in rearranging the cutlery at the side of her plate.

Her husband, however, seconded Dane's view. "Me, either."

Ali exhaled sharply in frustration. "Look, my personal life is not the issue here and neither is Luke Banning. The resort's future is what's important right now."

Dane, always the voice of reason, smiled and nodded. "I couldn't agree more."

Ali returned his smile, glad to have him on her side

in this matter. That made it two Conlans to one. End of discussion. She picked up her coffee cup and had just taken a sip when he added, "I think the resort needs Luke Banning."

Somehow she managed to choke down the hot liquid, but an undignified coughing fit ensued. When it had passed enough for her finally to speak, she demanded, "How can you say that, Dane?"

"We need another investor, Ali. It's as simple as that. If we want to buy that extra acreage when it comes on the market and put in a championship-caliber golf course and clubhouse, we need more capital. So our choices are either take out a loan to finance the expansion or take on another partner."

"There is a third option," Audra interjected sweetly before winking at Ali. "I could bankroll it."

Ali felt her lip curl at the suggestion. Audra knew Ali wouldn't allow her sister to sink any more of her vast personal wealth into their three-way partnership.

"Don't even go there, Aud. We've discussed it before. The answer is still no."

Glancing at her sister, Ali wondered again how it was possible for two people who had once shared a womb to turn out so differently. Not just physically, although even in that regard they were night and day. Audra was a blue-eyed bombshell of a blonde who had more curves than should be legal, while Ali was tawny-eyed, brunette and athletically slender. They barely looked like siblings let alone twins. In temperament, though, they were even more divergent. Ali was generally the more sedate, studious and practical of the pair. She left being flamboyant, frivolous and outrageous to Audra. In fairness, though, her sister was really none of those things any longer.

Since returning to Trillium Island a year earlier after a life-altering and nearly life-ending event, Audra had become much more subdued and centered. Now she was also much happier thanks to her recent marriage to Seth Ridley.

Audra and Ali had ended a decade-long estrangement, and Ali was delighted to have her sister back. Even so, the two women managed to lock horns on everything from fashion to politics.

Differences aside, though, Ali knew Audra and Dane were right about Saybrook's. If they hoped to make the resort not just profitable once again, but to put it back on the map as a hot vacation destination, then they needed a golf course. It was the only way to compete with the upscale mainland resorts that had lured away so much of Saybrook's business over the past decade.

A bigger investment from Audra was out of the question if the Conlans's business venture was to remain on relatively equal footing. As it was, Audra had sunk in more money than either one of her siblings.

A loan wasn't in their best interests either since the economy remained soft, gas prices were up and the experts were already predicting traffic would be down when the summer tourist season officially kicked off at the end of the month.

"We need another investor," Dane said quietly.

Ali sighed in defeat. "I know we do, but Banning? Does it have to be him?"

Dane shrugged.

"When we first talked about this idea, we agreed we wanted someone with ties to Trillium Island. Someone who would appreciate Saybrook's charm, as well as its importance not only to the island's history but to its overall economy. Luke fits the bill, especially since he's done very well for himself since leaving," he said patiently.

"I know."

Of course she did. Not because the man who'd broken her heart had called or written to her, but because she couldn't pick up a magazine or turn on the nightly news without seeing just what a huge success he'd become.

Dane wasn't finished driving the point home.

"Luke Banning's name on this project will give Saybrook's the kind of international exposure it hasn't had since the resort's heyday in the 1940s and 1950s when members of the Rat Pack and other Hollywood legends made it their Midwest destination."

"I thought that was part of Audra's appeal," Ali said nastily.

But her twin didn't rise to the bait. "I'm old news,

sweetie. Now that I'm married and haven't appeared on a tabloid cover in nearly a year, I'm a has-been."

Audra grinned at her husband of three months after saying it, clearly pleased to be passé after nearly a decade of generating headlines with her infamous antics.

Ali damned herself for being so practical. Their arguments made perfect sense, and if it weren't for her personal history with Luke, she would be the first to suggest approaching him. The fight had nearly gone out of Ali, but she decided to make one last stand.

"Who's to say Luke will want to have anything to do with the island? He left here more than a decade ago and has been pretty happy to stay away from it since then," she pointed out. "Now that he's such a big shot, he's probably forgotten all about this place. It certainly doesn't hold many happy memories for him given his childhood."

Dane cleared his throat and glanced toward Audra, who said, "Luke's interested."

"You've spoken to him?" Ali's incredulous gaze cut to her twin. "So this family dinner to discuss the future of the resort is really just a formality. You and Dane made the decision for Conlan Corporation behind my back."

"Not behind your back, Ali. We...um, actually, *I* made a phone call to Luke about a month ago and merely tossed the idea out to him," Audra said. "He got back to me a couple weeks ago, having decided the idea has merit, at which point I told him I needed to discuss it with the pair of you before things could go any further. I discussed it with Dane last week and now we're discussing it with you."

"You guys talked about this last week and you're just now getting around to clueing me in? How thoughtful," Ali muttered.

"I can always call Luke back and tell him you can't handle the idea of doing business with him," Audra offered.

Ali's vision blurred red once again.

"I can handle doing business with him," she snapped. "Although I doubt I'll actually have to. I'm sure Mr. Entrepreneur of the Year will delegate this project to some minion or another. We might not speak to him other than a conference call every now and then."

She was feeling better already about the prospect. Surely a businessman of Luke Banning's stature would not jet in from New York City to dirty his hands with a project as relatively small as this one, even if sentiment apparently had him opening his wallet to help finance it.

"So, it's agreed," Dane said. "The Conlan Corporation is offering Luke Banning a stake in the resort."

Ali begrudgingly grunted her consent while Audra flashed a triumphant smile.

It wasn't until Ali was pulling on her jacket at the end of the evening that Audra said, "By the way, the meeting will be a week from Wednesday."

"What meeting?"

"The meeting with Luke. That was the earliest he could get here to look over our plans for the golf course and clubhouse."

Ali didn't waste her breath giving voice to the scathing retort that came to mind. She banged out the side door and was in her car before Dane could rush after her and attempt to play peacemaker.

"I think that went rather well," Audra said, grinning at her brother as they stood by the side door and watched Ali's car speed up the long driveway that led back to the main road.

"Yeah," he replied dryly. "No one's bleeding."

Audra's thoughts turned to Luke Banning. "Not yet anyway."

CHAPTER ONE

THE sun was hot for mid-May, but Ali tipped back her head as she knelt in the small flower bed that ringed her mailbox and took a moment to enjoy the way it felt on her face. Northern Michigan's winters were always long, especially when lake-effect storms were added in. This winter had felt interminable. Just a few weeks earlier the last of the snow had finally melted from the woods that bordered the northern edge of her property. Trillium, the three-petaled flower for which the Lake Michigan island was named, bloomed there now, offering a much warmer carpet of white.

It was Sunday, which meant she had just three days to reconcile herself to seeing Luke again. She *was* over him, no matter what Audra seemed to think. But he'd been Ali's first love, which made him impossible to forget. And he'd left her behind after three years of dating without a second thought, which made his desertion impossible to forgive. So of course the prospect of seeing him again had her on edge. That was only natural.

It didn't help that Audra had ideas for this reunion that clearly went beyond business. In the past week, her twin had hinted broadly that Ali might want to do something with the shoulder-length hair she always wore pulled into a simple ponytail. And she had tried to convince Ali to wear more fashionable clothing than the conservative button-down blouses and straight, below-the-knee skirts that populated her wardrobe.

Ali ignored the unsolicited advice. This was business, not a social call. She wasn't going to doll herself up for Luke Banning's return. No, indeed.

Indifference, that's what Wednesday's meeting called for. Nonchalance.

Ali yanked a weed out of the flower bed and tossed it atop the small heap of wilting interlopers next to her, warming to her strategy.

She would be ruthlessly polite and exceedingly casual when she and Luke were finally face-to-face. She would show him, Audra and everyone else who thought otherwise that the past was ancient history, and that the fact he'd spent the past decade in New York City growing wealthy and respected and enjoying the tabloid-documented attentions of supermodels and liposuctioned socialites was of absolutely no concern to her.

She snatched up her gardening trowel and hacked at the hard ground with its daggerlike metal point.

On Wednesday, she would be professional and businesslike. She would be cordial, but in a detached—*hack! hack!*—and disinterested—*hack! hack!*—way.

She swiped at the sweat beading on her brow and then set aside the trowel so she could wrap her fist around the base of another weed. As she knelt there locked in an intense tug-of-war with a deep-rooted dandelion, she heard the motorcycle. The mere sound of the engine reeled her back in time, as it always did, resurrecting the bittersweet memories she'd just convinced herself were safely buried and of no threat to her emotional well-being.

Even as her heart seemed to kick out an extra beat, she told herself she was being foolish. It wasn't Luke. *It couldn't be Luke.* She still had three days, nearly seventy-two hours, before she would see him again. Besides, he wouldn't still be driving a damned motorcycle after all these years. He probably traveled in a limousine, a stretch one so long it would barely fit on the ferry that brought vehicles over from the mainland.

But as she shielded her eyes from the sun with one grimy hand, a Harley Davidson Sportster crested the hill and rumbled into view.

In the years he'd been gone, sightings of Trillium Island's most famous son seemed to be about as common as sightings of Elvis, and they'd proved to be as reliable. There was no mistaking the Harley rider's identity, though, especially since he was flouting state law by forgoing a helmet.

Even with the space of thirty yards and the span of more than a decade separating them, Ali knew him at a glance. Wind ruffled the almost-black hair she'd once run her fingers through. He was wearing it shorter these days, looking more like a respectable adult than the rowdy teenager and young man he'd been. Aviator sunglasses obscured his eyes, but she remembered that they were the same shade of blue as the cool waters of the great lake that surrounded the island.

A dozen feet from her driveway the bike slowed and all hope that Luke would somehow fail to spot her evaporated.

Indifference, she reminded herself.

Disinterest.

Nonchalance.

And yet all she felt was mule-kicked when he brought the bike to a stop in front of her mailbox, grinning for a long moment in that sexy way that had haunted her dreams and taunted her heart.

Finally he switched off the engine and swung one denim-encased leg over the seat.

"Hi."

The sparseness of his greeting jolted her back to her senses. He'd been gone nearly a dozen years and the first word out of his mouth was *hi?* She wasn't sure what she had expected him to say, but he didn't even have the decency to look contrite or uncomfortable or babble his way through an apology, which she would of course decline to accept. No. He was smiling, as handsome and overconfident as ever, and acting as if he hadn't sped away on that same damned Harley more than a decade earlier without so much as a backward glance.

Studying him, Ali wondered what she had ever seen in the man…beyond his staggering good looks. Those, she noted sourly, had only improved with age. It wasn't fair. He should be balding or overweight, but the photographic images she'd seen of him over the years hadn't been airbrushed or otherwise doctored. His hair was still thick, his physique lean and muscled, and his face chiseled and gorgeous.

It dawned on her then that she was still on her knees gazing up at him like the same starry-eyed girl whose heart he'd broken.

Pride fired Ali to her feet. She wiped her soiled hands on her jeans and inwardly cursed her habit of not wearing gardening gloves. There was no help for her dirty cuticles or her perspiration-damp appearance beneath the ball cap she wore, but she damn well wouldn't kneel like some supplicant before Luke Banning of all people.

"Hello."

To her relief her voice sounded normal, its tone just this side of cool, but he was smiling as if he thought she were delighted that he'd rumbled down her lane, disturbing her peace and nature's quiet on this sunny Sunday afternoon.

"God, you look the same as I remembered…give or take a dirt smudge."

Laughing, he reached out and touched her cheek, presumably to wipe away some errant soil. His smile dimmed when Ali backed up a step and crossed her arms over her chest.

"Believe me, I've changed."

"I guess we all have." He slipped off the glasses and she felt lost in those blue eyes until he added, "Ten years will do that."

"It's been eleven."

He nodded and one side of his mouth crooked up. "Eleven. How have you been, Ali?"

"Fine."

"I read in the paper last year that Audra had married again. When I spoke to her on the telephone a couple weeks ago, she seemed very happy."

"Yes. Apparently the fourth time is the charm," Ali replied. And because the words seemed somehow disloyal given the vast metamorphosis her twin had gone through, she added, "Seth's a great guy. I think this one will stick."

"I'm glad for her. What about you? Anybody special in your life these days?"

She hadn't expected him to come right out and ask her such a personal question, and so she spluttered, "I— I'm seeing someone."

Did one date actually count as "seeing"? Bradley had asked her out again since then, twice in fact. But she'd put him off. Standing in front of Luke, she decided there was really no reason she shouldn't take Bradley up on his offer of dinner the following Saturday.

"Is he an islander?"

"No. In fact, he's relatively new to the area. He lives on the mainland, just outside Petoskey."

Luke nodded. "Speaking of the mainland, there's a lot of new development along the waterfront. I barely recognized parts of it when I flew over."

When Ali glanced in bafflement at his bike, Luke caressed the motorcycle's handlebars. On a shrug he said, "One of the perks of having my own aircraft is that I always have room for my Harley."

His priorities apparently hadn't changed, but she kept that thought to herself. No reason to dredge up the past. Indeed, she planned to keep the conversation as impersonal as possible.

"Those new developments on the mainland are giving Saybrook's some stiff competition, which is why we want to buy the property adjacent to the resort and add a golf course as soon as we can manage it."

Luke shook his head and grinned again. "I still can't believe you guys bought the resort."

The comment rankled, so much so that her determination to remain impersonal began to waver. After all, he wasn't the only one who had made something of himself. Ali had graduated cum laude with a degree in business and was now part owner of one of the Midwest's most storied resorts.

"It's prime real estate and despite the fact that the previous manager drove it to the brink of bankruptcy, it's already starting to rebound," she said. "A couple of good seasons and we'll be operating in the black. But then I'm sure you already know that or you wouldn't be considering entering into a partnership with us."

"I'm not questioning the soundness of the investment," Luke said, holding up a hand. "It's just that back when we were kids who would have guessed that the Conlans would someday own Saybrook's?"

"Yes, and who would have guessed that a high school dropout would go on to be called Entrepreneur of the Year by a respected national business journal?" she replied.

The words came out snide rather than tinged with the begrudging admiration she felt. Ali could tell Luke realized that. He slipped his sunglasses back on, his happy-go-lucky grin receding into a taut line of compressed lips.

"Yeah. I guess the kids at Trillium High who voted me most likely to wind up incarcerated are eating their words about now. Makes me almost sorry I didn't make it for the last class reunion."

Ali felt too small for reminding him of his rocky adolescence to point out that since he hadn't graduated, technically he would not have been invited to any of his class's reunions.

"That was a long time ago," she murmured, realizing even as she said it that she certainly hadn't let go of the past.

It was a moment before Luke broke the awkward silence. "I did get my diploma, you know."

She blinked in surprise as much at his words as at the quiet pride with which they were spoken. He'd dropped out of high school during his senior year, and although Ali was three years his junior and they hadn't started to date until she was nearly a senior herself, his lack of a diploma had been the cause of more than a few arguments. She had urged him repeatedly to go back to night school or earn a general equivalency degree. He was too smart not to, she'd told him.

"I didn't know," she said. Then, "I'm glad."

"I took adult education courses after I left. It didn't take me very long."

"What made you decide to do it?"

He shrugged and glanced away. "It was just after I'd made my first million with the dot-com I'd founded. I guess I didn't want people to think I was a fluke or... stupid."

"I never thought you were stupid."

"No." The grin was back in a flash of white teeth. "You just thought I was reckless and impulsive. I still am, by the way."

And because the grin had sent a shower of sparks through her system, she retorted crisply, "I can tell. You're driving that damned Harley without a helmet. That's illegal, you know."

"Not in every state. Besides, you can't get the full experience with a bucket strapped to your head." A pair of dark brows rose over the top rim of the sunglasses. "Want to go for a ride, Ali? I can go real slow if you'd like, or take you fast."

His silky tone and the double entendre implied along with his raised brows had gooseflesh appearing on her arms.

"Fast or slow, I never liked your bike," she answered primly.

"No. But you used to like me."

What she'd felt had gone a great deal beyond "like," and he damned well knew it. Ali notched up her chin and let the chill seep into her inflection when she said, "So, what are you doing all the way out here today?"

She asked, but she thought she knew. Surely he had driven to this secluded shore of the island to speak with her in private before the midweek meeting at which Dane and Audra would be present. An apology would be coming any minute…an apology she still planned to decline.

Ali's stone cottage, which had once belonged to her grandmother, sat on Trillium's western shore, affording it a breathtaking view of Lake Michigan. It was tucked in amid a huge parcel of state land, making it the only private residence for miles. The only private residence except for…

Even before she could finish the thought, Luke was pointing to the slight rise at the northern edge of her property. Since the leaves on the trees were still sparse,

Ali could just make out the pitch of the neighboring cottage's roof and she cursed her hubris.

The place had belonged to Luke's grandmother. Elsie Banning had raised Luke after his father, an alcoholic, had died while Luke was still in grade school. Luke's mother had already abandoned the family by then. As Elsie's only surviving kin, the cottage and the seven wooded acres on which it sat technically belonged to Luke.

"I thought I'd swing by the old house and see how it's fared since I've been gone." He took off his sunglasses again and fiddled with the ear pieces. Regret colored his tone when he added, "I should have had someone taking care of it over the years."

Elsie had died just three months before he'd left Trillium. If the man had one redeeming trait, Ali knew it was that he'd loved his grandmother without reserve. Her death had devastated him.

"I've looked in on it from time to time," she admitted.

She'd done more than that, actually. She'd kept the grass mowed, the carpet roses trimmed back and the cobblestone path that led from the driveway to the front door free of weeds. She'd done it for Elsie, not for Luke, or at least that's what she'd told herself. But sometimes, after finishing the yard work, she would sit on the rear porch that faced the big lake, rock slowly back and forth in the wide swing where she and Luke had long ago shared their first taste of passion, and wonder what he was doing and if he ever thought about her.

The fact that he'd run into her today by accident seemed to answer that question now.

"I appreciate it," he said.

"It's no trouble to walk over," she replied on a shrug.

Luke motioned toward the house behind her. "Does that mean you live here now?"

She nodded. "My grandmother deeded it to me when she moved to Florida with my parents six years ago."

He smiled slowly and despite Ali's closed posture, laid one warm hand on her upper arm and squeezed. The casual contact caused her traitorous pulse to shoot off like a bottle rocket and had her irritated all over again. He seemed not to notice, lost as he was in reminiscing.

"I think I spent as much time in your grandmother's kitchen as I did in my own. She made the best sugar cookies on Trillium. Remember how when we were kids we would sneak them off the baking tray before they even had a chance to cool?"

Ali didn't want to be reminded of the ways in which their lives had once twined together so sweetly since his abandonment had caused her heart to fray apart afterward. And so when he asked, "How is Mrs. Conlan doing these days?" she announced baldly, "She died last winter."

"God, I'm sorry." He slipped the glasses back on, making Ali wonder if she had just imagined that fleeting shadow of what had looked like self-reproach. "I didn't know."

"How would you?"

"Ali." He said her name quietly, and then stroked her cheek. This time she didn't back away, if only to prove to herself that his touch meant nothing.

A bee buzzed past and overhead a blue jay's shrill cry rent the silence as they regarded one another.

Finally, motioning in the direction of his grandmother's property, Ali said, "Don't let me keep you, Luke. I know you're a busy and important man."

He hesitated, and she thought for a moment he was going to say something, but then he dropped his hand and straddled the bike, firing it to life with a swift downward kick of his booted foot. Over the engine's throaty growl he hollered, "See you Wednesday."

Wednesday, Ali knew, would come much too soon.

Luke slowed the bike as he approached the driveway to his grandmother's cottage, but in the end, he sped past it, instead following the rutted road as it wound through the woods and then spilled back onto the main drag a dozen miles later.

He hadn't felt up to seeing the cottage and confronting any more of his past. Not after seeing Ali.

He'd known her right away. She hadn't changed much. Even the baseball cap snugged over her crown was the same. He snorted out a laugh that was lost to the wind. The woman just couldn't give up on the Detroit Tigers even though they hadn't won a World Series since 1984.

Despite her poor taste in baseball teams, she looked good. Better than good, actually, even with her dark hair sprouting from the back of the cap, perspiration dotting her upper lip and dirt streaking her right cheek. Her eyes were still a couple shades darker than caramel and she'd kept her figure, that long-legged, slim-hipped athletic build that had given him many a sleepless night in his youth.

He frowned, realizing that none of the women he'd dated during the past decade had looked anything like her. There had been blondes and redheads, but not a single brunette. Certainly none of those women had been a fan of baseball much less able to pitch one low and inside while the bases were loaded in the bottom of the ninth.

That had been only one of Ali's talents, of course. Remembering the others nearly had him crashing his bike into the unforgiving trunk of a sugar maple.

He'd thought he'd forgotten her. No, that wasn't true. He'd *never* forgotten her. But over the years he'd convinced himself that adolescence and inexperience had magnified and romanticized the feelings he'd once had for her. In a way, she'd been the girl next door, since their grandmothers had lived side by side. He and Ali had always known one another and hung around together since Luke and her older brother, Dane, had been good friends.

Then, the summer she was seventeen, the pigtails he'd once pulled had become the sleek tumble of hair he'd weaved his fingers through. God, he still remembered the magic of that first kiss and the way her slim arms had wrapped around him and held tight when he would have backed away. He'd been twenty at the time and Luke had known that everyone on the island, including her family, thought their match was a mistake.

Looking back now, he didn't blame them. He'd had no prospects at all, just big dreams as he'd pumped gas for the luxury cabin cruisers that stopped at Whitey's Marina. Ali, on the other hand, was set to graduate top in her class and had plans to go away for her degree after completing a couple years at the community college on the mainland to save money.

He'd always figured his leaving had been as much a favor to her as a way out for him. Despite being accepted at the University of Michigan a few hours' drive downstate, she'd begun to talk about staying on Trillium, taking correspondence courses or transferring to a less prestigious university near Traverse City and commuting a couple days of the week. Both of their futures had seemed so doomed.

Then his grandmother had died.

Luke could still hear the words Elsie Banning had spoken to him as she lay in a hospital bed, hooked up to an assortment of beeping, buzzing machines.

She'd gripped his hand with her knobby fingers and in a voice barely above a whisper she'd commanded, "Be happy, Luke, and make me proud. You're not your father. It breaks my heart to see you settle for being less than what you were meant to be."

Even now, her words drove him. He revved the bike's engine, catching air as he crested another hill. Before touching down again on the other side he caught a glimpse of the big lake glittering in the midday sun. His grandmother had always loved that lake and the limitless potential she said she saw in its sheer vastness.

"I've made something of myself!" He shouted the words as he raced against the long shadows of his past.

At thirty-four, he enjoyed the distinction of being one of the few dot-comers who'd gotten rich and then wisely gotten out before the bubble burst. Since then he'd invested in more traditional ventures, primarily real estate, cultivating a reputation as a shrewd dealmaker. He'd accomplished every goal he'd set and exceeded even his own very high expectations.

He was Luke Banning, successful businessman, respected entrepreneur. No one pitied him now or looked askance at him when he walked into a room. Hell, people paid him large sums of money and sat shoulder to shoulder in crowded auditoriums just for the privilege of hearing him share his expertise.

"I've made something of myself," he shouted again, wondering why his triumphant return to Trillium didn't feel quite as sweet as he'd imagined it would.

And wondering why it was that for all he had accumulated over the years something still seemed to be missing.

CHAPTER TWO

ALI thumbed through the clothes in her closet once again. Even though Audra wasn't in the room, she swore that every time she selected something, she heard her twin whispering, "You're not going to wear that, are you?"

And so it was that with a mere forty minutes before the Conlans were to meet with Luke Banning, Ali found herself standing in her bra and panties, and dithering between a navy skirt and a black skirt that were the exact same conservative cut and by the same maker.

Gazing at the garments, she muttered aloud, "When did I become so damned boring?"

Exasperated, she tossed both skirts onto the small mountain of clothes on her bed and stuffed her arm into the far reaches of the cramped closet. After a minute of fruitless fishing, she finally produced what she was looking for: A suit the color of freshly spilled blood.

The jacket cut in sharply at the waist and then fell

away at the hip. As for the skirt, it was a little shorter than the rest of her closet's offerings. Instead of ending primly just below the knee, it skimmed to the middle of her thighs. She'd bought it on sale last fall while shopping with Audra, which explained the vivid color and more daring cut. She'd planned to take it back. In fact, the tags still dangled from one sleeve. Now she was glad she'd kept it. Black, tan and navy just didn't suit her mood today.

Blood-red did.

Half an hour later, she stood in front of the full-length mirror that was affixed to the back of her bedroom door and surveyed her appearance.

None of this, she assured herself, was for Luke's benefit. She'd been thinking about making some changes, paying a little more attention to small details like putting on eyeliner and a faint sweep of blush to highlight her cheekbones.

Besides, she didn't want the man thinking that all she owned were blue jeans and ball caps. She wanted him to see her as a professional and an equal. And okay, she could admit it. She wanted him to see her as a woman… a woman who was off-limits.

She'd left her hair loose. She couldn't remember the last time she hadn't yanked it all back in some sort of clip or another. When they were girls, she had envied Audra her wild tumble of curls. The grass always being greener, her sister had complained mightily that Ali had lucked out with her stick-straight mane. Today, Ali had to admit, she rather liked the way it fell to her shoulders in a sleek cascade the same color as the antique mahogany bureau that had once belonged to her grandmother.

The suit fit as well as she remembered, accentuating curves she hadn't known she possessed. She would die a slow and painful death before admitting it to Audra, but Ali really liked the way it looked and the way it made her feel: professional and put together, with the side bonus of sexiness.

Then she glanced down at her shoes. The serviceable black pumps with the rounded toe looked like something an arthritic grandmother would wear now that they were matched with a chic suit and a white silk blouse.

She didn't want to do it, but Ali finally broke down. Picking up the telephone, she dialed Audra's number, praying that her perennially late sibling had not become suddenly punctual and already left for the resort. A breathless Audra picked up on the fourth ring.

"Aud, you haven't left." She sighed in relief.

"I'm on my way, I swear. Practically out the door as we speak. Seth just…and then I…" She trailed off on a throaty laugh that made words unnecessary. Ali swore she felt herself blush.

"Newlyweds," she muttered. "Don't go into detail. *Please.* I have neither the time nor the inclination to listen to a play-by-play. I need a favor."

"A favor? What kind of a favor?" Audra asked.

"I'm having a bit of…a problem," Ali hedged. Then, "Oh, hell, I need to borrow a pair of pumps."

"You're having a shoe emergency? God, I love it." Laughter bubbled through the phone line. "I suppose it would be small of me to remind you that last month when I showed off the new pair of Kate Spades I'd purchased, you asked how many feet I had that I needed another pair of shoes."

"I knew calling you would be a mistake," Ali snapped.

Audra wasn't insulted at all. "No, sweetie, *not* calling would have been the mistake. I may have changed my life around and gotten rid of a lot of the fluff, but I still have more fashion sense in my pinky than you'll ever have in your entire bony body."

Damn, Ali thought, wasn't that the pathetic truth.

"So, will you help?"

Audra made a dismissive sound. "Of course I will. What are you going to wear?"

"The suit I bought when I went shopping downstate with you last fall."

"The red one?" Audra whistled low. "Good choice and aren't you glad I talked you into buying it?" Before Ali could answer, her sister was saying, "Please tell me you didn't pair it with one of those starched oxfords you seem to own stock in?"

"No. I do have a white silk blouse." Exactly one, and again it had been purchased while out with Audra.

"Could we get back to shoes? All I have are the black pumps I normally wear to work."

Through the receiver came Audra's low moan. "How can we be sisters let alone twins?"

"Aud, the minutes are ticking away here. I really don't have time for a discussion on DNA. What have you got for me?"

"Let me think about it. I'll go hunt through my closet and see what I can come up with. Come straight to my office when you get to the resort."

"I'll be there in fifteen. And, Aud?"

"Yeah?"

"Thanks for not rubbing it in too much."

Her sister snorted. "Who says I'm done?"

Luke had already seen Ali since returning to Trillium, so he didn't expect their meeting today to be awkward. Then, recalling the cool way in which she had regarded him during their chance encounter on Sunday, he amended his opinion. It probably still would be awkward, but not as awkward as it could have been had they not already come face-to-face.

But then she walked into the conference room decked out in red and exposing a pair of long, toned legs that any Rockette would be proud to insure, and he nearly forgot how to breathe.

Who was *this* woman?

Three days ago, Ali had looked almost unchanged to

him wearing a ball cap and faded jeans, with no makeup on her face and her hair pulled back the way she'd always worn it. He'd found comfort in that fact and, when he'd had a chance to think about it, it made his lingering attraction to her understandable, maybe even a little nostalgic.

He wasn't feeling nostalgic now, or comfortable. When she rolled back her shoulders to let the jacket slip down her silk-covered arms, he shifted in his seat and had to stifle a groan. No, he wasn't feeling comfortable at all.

"Hello, Luke."

They were alone in the room. Dane had just gone to take a phone call and Audra had yet to arrive. Luke stood because the moment seemed to require him to be on his feet. Once he was upright, he hastily pulled closed his suit jacket, more than a little appalled by his body's embarrassing reaction.

The other day when he'd come upon Ali as she'd knelt pulling weeds, he had enjoyed the advantage of surprise. Today, the shoe was on the other foot—and what a sexy little number it was, too, black and open-toed, allowing a tantalizing peek at red-painted nails. God help him, but he'd always had a thing about women's feet. And this woman, he remembered, had a very sensitive instep.

As his gaze connected with hers, something about the way her lips twitched told Luke she knew she had him shaken...and stirred.

"You clean up well," he admitted.

"Thank you." One slim dark eyebrow notched up when she added, "I try to dress for the occasion."

He nodded, wondering just what he should infer from her bold color choice this day. And then, because he wanted badly to touch her and test himself, he held out his hand.

A long moment passed before she reached to shake it. At the contact, Luke felt the wild sizzle he thought he had either outgrown or simply imagined.

"Some things never change," he murmured, taking a step closer.

She pulled her hand free, stepped back. "And some things do."

He acknowledged her words with a nod. She was different and the same all at once, the girl he remembered wrapped in the body of an alluring and mysterious woman.

An alluring and mysterious woman who was all business when she said, "Why don't you have a seat? Dane and Audra should be along shortly."

"Okay."

"More coffee?" she asked, as she reached for the insulated carafe and mugs that were on a tray in the middle of the table. Her blouse fell open a little as she leaned forward and reached, affording him a fleeting glimpse of something lacy and white and the gentle swell of flesh that disappeared inside it. He sucked in a breath, drawing her attention.

"Everything all right?" she asked, those not-quite-brown, not-quite-gold eyes narrowing.

"Fine." Then Luke couldn't resist. He let his gaze dip down again and said with a little more emphasis, "Very fine."

She straightened instantly, her posture rigid as she filled her coffee cup to the top and then slid into the seat opposite his. She didn't bother with cream or sugar, he noted. He got the feeling if she were to walk into one of the trendy coffee shops in Manhattan she would bypass all of the frothy concoctions listed on the order board and go for plain French roast. She'd always been practical. As he studied her, she snagged a handful of dark hair and tucked it behind her ear and out of the way. That move was practical, too, but that didn't make it any less sexy.

"I'm sure you've had a chance to read through our plans for the golf course. I'm curious to hear what you think," she said.

Business, Luke reminded himself. That's why he was here. And so he straightened in his seat and decided to get down to it.

"Three hundred acres is ample space for a course the size you're talking about, but if we could pick up additional acreage we could make the holes relatively secluded from one another. We could leave in a lot more trees that way, too. It makes for a picturesque experience and golfers appreciate not having to worry about hearing 'Fore!' hollered while they're in the middle of their back swing."

"How much land are you talking?"

"Another hundred acres would be ideal."

"What's this about another hundred acres?" Dane asked as he walked through the door. Audra was right behind him, her face breaking into a grin even before she had cleared the threshold.

Where Ali had acknowledged Luke with cool reserve, Audra wrapped him in a hug and gave him a smacking kiss on the lips.

"It's good to see you, Luke."

"Good to see you, too." And he meant it. He suddenly realized how much he'd missed this place and these people.

Dane had been his best friend since grade school, remaining such despite some tense moments after Luke and Ali had started dating. He'd always figured Dane didn't think Luke was good enough for his sister, even though Dane had never come right out and said it. Even so, they'd stayed tight. That their friendship had fallen by the wayside, another casualty of his leaving, was Luke's fault, and he knew it. Dane's cool greeting when Luke arrived on Trillium told Luke he knew it, too.

As for Audra, she'd always been a kindred spirit. Luke had never fantasized about her, despite her Marilyn Monroe curves and come-hither smile, the way he'd fantasized about Ali. Clasping Audra's hand now, he didn't feel that crazy current of electricity shoot up his arm, either, just the pleasant warmth of remembered friendship.

"Sorry I couldn't get by to see you before now, but Seth and I have been pretty busy," she said.

"Newlyweds usually are," Luke teased.

A glimpse of Ali's tight expression told him she wasn't all that pleased with her twin's enthusiastic greeting. Given the fact that Audra had been on the back of his Harley when he left Trillium, as eager as he to get the hell out, he figured he understood that. And still, he couldn't keep from hugging her back.

Dane's exclamation ended Luke's reverie.

"Whoa, Al, look at you!" Dane whistled. Luke couldn't be sure but he thought Audra poked her brother in the ribs, after which Dane coughed and said, "I mean, I've always liked that outfit."

Ali flushed, but then settled back into her chair. After taking a sip of her coffee, she said, "Luke was mentioning that he thought if we could add some acreage to the golf course, it might make it more aesthetically pleasing."

"And safer for golfers," Luke inserted. "Insurance premiums being what they are, that's something to take into consideration."

"But another hundred acres," Dane began, pulling out the plat map from the stack of files he'd brought with him. "Where would we pick up that kind of land?"

"It doesn't have to be a single parcel," Luke said, following Dane to the table.

He stood just between Ali and Dane's chairs and his arm brushed her shoulder when he leaned over for a better look at the map. He was wearing cologne, the same crisp yet subtle scent he'd always favored. It had Ali inhaling deeply and remembering. She forced her attention back to the map. They had shaded in the acreage they planned to purchase. It was a sizable tract that snaked along one edge of the resort's property line.

"Do the Dohertys still own this chunk of land?" Luke asked, tapping his finger on a pie-shaped chunk.

"Yes and they're not budging," Audra commented. She leaned one hip on the table on the opposite side of Dane and sighed. "We've already dangled the carrot."

"There's a rumor that the Tollmans are interested in getting rid of the thirty-five acres behind their beachfront cottage," Dane said. "A good portion of it is wetland, though."

"For a golf course, you need to think of it as a hazard, not a wetland," Luke said, smiling. "Do you think some of it might be usable?"

Before her brother could answer, Ali gave voice to the idea that had been kicking around in her head since the conversation began.

"What if in addition to the acreage we're planning to purchase, we use part of the resort's property?" She angled in her seat so she could look at Luke. One glance at those liquid eyes nearly had her forgetting what she was planning to say.

"Go on," he coaxed and his gaze dipped to her lips as if in anticipation of the words.

"We—we've been thinking of adding half a dozen cottages in the woods. I was just thinking, what if we reconfigured the entire setup of the resort's existing three hundred acres, factoring in the golf course and the additional land? We could give some of the old cottages fairway views and add new structures to some of the other holes once the course is complete."

His eyebrows notched up and then he grinned in a way that stole her breath.

"Do you play?" he asked.

"Excuse me?"

"Golf. Do you play?"

"I don't really have time for games," she replied even though she did indeed play. She could feel her face heating under his scrutiny and knew without looking that her sister was smiling smugly and Dane had crossed his arms over his chest.

"Pity." Luke shrugged. "Life's not much fun without a little recreation. What do you do to relax?"

"I work."

"Hmm. I wonder what your boyfriend thinks about that?"

"Her boyfriend?" Audra blurted out.

"Bradley Townsend isn't…bothered in the least by the fact that I enjoy my job," Ali replied.

None of it was a lie. She hadn't called him her boyfriend. And during their one date he hadn't complained at all about her demanding career.

"Are you going to see Townsend again?" Dane asked.

"Saturday." She cleared her throat. "Can we get back to business? Please."

Luke straightened and walked back around to his chair. "I like the idea," he said, settling onto the seat. "The reason I asked if you played golf, Ali, is I think you hit a hole-in-one with that plan."

She flushed again, this time for a very different reason. She almost hated herself for it. What did it matter what he thought of her? She wasn't out to please Luke Banning. She crossed her legs, tugged at the hem of her skirt and tried to convince herself she wasn't lying.

Three hours later, Luke and the Conlans emerged from the room with a partnership forged and their signatures drying on the thick stack of paperwork their various lawyers had had a hand in drawing up.

"When will you be heading back to New York?" Audra asked.

Luke had planned to leave Trillium that afternoon. He had two meetings scheduled in Manhattan on Friday and plans to attend an exhibit at the Metropolitan Museum of Art with Rochelle Bullard on Saturday.

Now, the thought of returning to his penthouse held no appeal. He told himself it was just that he hadn't had much time off in recent months. He was due a vacation and, besides, he'd never made it out to his grandmother's cottage. He should check on it and then look into putting it on the market.

The thought of selling it made him unexpectedly sad. He wasn't a sentimental man. In business, he couldn't afford to be. In his personal life, he just plain didn't care to be. His relationship with Rochelle, for instance, was casual and hardly headed in the direction of serious. He glanced at Ali and wondered if her date with the developer on Saturday would end with a chaste peck or a sweaty tussle between the sheets. He felt a muscle tick in his cheek at the disturbing visual his thoughts conjured up.

In response to Audra's question he heard himself say, "I haven't decided when I'll leave."

Ali sat on the rear deck of her cottage that evening and watched the setting sun shimmer in hues of pink of gold over Lake Michigan. Dane and Audra had gone to dinner with Luke. Seth would be meeting them. Ali had made excuses and headed for home, eager for some time alone.

As soon as she'd walked through the cottage's door, she'd poured herself a glass of wine, turned on some vintage Bonnie Raitt and shed her clothes along with Audra's killer shoes. They'd looked great, but they had proved anything but comfortable.

Now, dressed in blue jeans and an oversize University of Michigan sweatshirt, she sipped merlot and thanked God that even before knowing Luke would be on Trillium, she had scheduled a couple of days off from the resort. She saw no reason to change her plans now. She wasn't a coward, but the less she saw of Luke Banning, the better.

Having made that determination, her gaze drifted down to the beach and she nearly bobbled her wine.

"Hey, Ali!" Luke called out, hiking up the grassy incline to the deck wearing a cocky grin that put her teeth on edge.

Wouldn't it just figure that she was back in jeans with her feet bare and her face scrubbed free of every last speck of foundation? She'd felt powerful and in control wearing that savvy red suit and a subtle touch of makeup. Now she felt like Cinderella must have after midnight struck. Damn the man, but he still looked like royalty even without the designer clothes he'd worn earlier. She had to admit, the suit had surprised her. Despite his wealth, she'd figured Luke would stroll in to their meeting wearing jeans. But he'd looked plenty at ease decked out in what she suspected was Armani.

"I thought you'd gone to dinner with Dane and Audra."

"I took a rain check."

"I didn't hear your motorcycle."

"Probably because your music's kind of loud." He grinned, nodding toward the house where Bonnie Raitt's sooty voice wailed from the speakers. Ali wanted to kick herself as she realized the singer was now crooning about how she couldn't make somebody love her.

She shrugged. "I always play my music loud. I don't have any neighbors to worry about."

"That could change," he said. But before she could ask what he meant, he was motioning toward the pastel-flooded horizon. "I'd forgotten how beautiful the sunsets are here."

"One of the reasons I could never see myself living anywhere else," she replied.

Even so, as she took another sip of her wine, she tried to be objective. She tried to see this small slice of the universe from Luke's perspective. She tried to understand for the millionth time what had made it so impossible for him to remain all those years before. She couldn't, though. Not then, and not now. And because of the way he stirred up her emotions Ali discovered that as much as she'd wanted him to stay when she was a naïve twenty-year-old, now she just wanted him to go away and leave her alone.

Luke didn't go away, though. He settled onto the top step that led to the deck, and then leaned back on his elbows. He was the picture of a man at leisure even as Ali felt wound up tight and ready to spring.

"Are the winters still as hard as I remember?" he asked.

"Worse."

"Kids still go sledding down Palmer Hill?"

"Yep."

She'd hoped by not contributing much to the conversation he would take the hint and leave, but he didn't appear to be put off by her laconic replies.

"Remember the time we crashed our toboggan into that oak tree near the bottom?" he asked, shaking his head and chuckling softly. "You were what, seven?"

"Eight. I still have the scar on the bottom of my chin

from the stitches. You, of course, walked away without a scratch. You have quite a talent for that."

He frowned and they fell silent for a moment. A crow called overhead and Luke looked up.

"It's quiet and loud here at the same time. A different kind of loud from the city. I didn't realize how much I missed that."

"Probably not a lot of crows in New York."

"Nope, pigeons."

He watched her raise the wineglass to her lips and then licked his own.

"You know, the neighborly thing would be to offer me some."

The hoarse sound that issued from the back of her throat was one of disbelief at his nerve. She hadn't invited him to join her and she thought she'd been making it clear she didn't want him to remain.

"I'm not feeling very neighborly."

"Your sainted grandmother would be appalled," he noted.

His comment grated because they both knew he was right. Gran would have slain the fatted calf to celebrate his return. She'd always had a soft spot for him.

"You've got a hell of a lot of nerve, Banning."

"Nah, what I've got is a powerful thirst." Luke's mouth curved in a lethal grin. "Please," he added.

"Anything to get you off of my deck," she muttered, standing. She handed him her wine. "Hold this."

"My pleasure," he replied. To her shocked dismay, he tipped up the glass and emptied the remaining wine in a single swallow.

Awareness jolted through her as she watched his lips cover the spot where hers had just been. She still remembered what those lips were capable of, and she was sure he'd had plenty of opportunity to hone his skill over the years.

"I can't believe you drank the rest of my wine," she sputtered, hoping indignation would camouflage that unwelcome spark of interest.

"Couldn't help myself," he said, rising slowly to his feet.

She held her ground even as he moved in and crowded her space.

"That's a handy excuse, isn't it?"

Luke shrugged. "Some things are impossible to resist. A good glass of wine." He twirled the goblet by its stem. "A beautiful woman."

His gaze connected with hers, one eyebrow lifting.

"Don't even think about it," she replied darkly.

"That sounds like a dare. I never could back down from a dare." His head was dipping, blue eyes blazing with a combination of interest and challenge. "Aren't you curious if it will be as good as you remember?" he asked.

"No."

"Liar," he said softly and then his mouth closed over hers.

CHAPTER THREE

ALI wanted to kill Luke. She wound up kissing him back instead. She leaned into his warmth, wrapped her arms around his solid frame and held on as her resolve wobbled and sensations both new and familiar swamped her.

Was the kiss as good as she remembered? Oh, no. It was better.

Much, much better.

To her way of thinking that was yet another reason to despise the man and hate herself.

She finally managed to infuse some steel into her spine and break away, but not before Luke nipped her bottom lip with his teeth, telegraphing need to every inch of her already aching body.

"Don't do that again," Ali panted. It was galling to realize she was breathing as hard as a sprinter who'd just set a new world record while crossing the finish line.

She thought Luke would smile. She waited for those skillful lips to curl with arrogance, but his mouth remained clamped in a grim line. Then he stepped back, set the wine glass on the arm of one of the deck's Adirondack chairs and, dipping his hands into the front pockets of his jeans, regarded her solemnly for a long moment.

"I'm sorry," he said at last.

Ali tilted up her chin in challenge. "For what? What are you sorry about, Luke?" she demanded.

He turned away from her, glancing out at the sunset. Limned in that subtle glow of gold he looked almost like a vision. How many times over the years had Ali imagined him standing on her doorstep? How many times had she conjured up this very conversation and waited for his apology? Was it *finally* forthcoming?

"I'm not sure," he said at last.

He faced her again and stepped closer. In the ebbing light of day she caught the glint of something dangerous in his gaze, which had drifted to her mouth. "You've gotten pretty good at that, by the way."

"Practice," she took delight in saying, even though she could count on one hand the number of men she'd dated in his absence. None of the relationships had lasted long or progressed very far, facts she was determined to keep to herself since none of that was his business.

"Practice makes perfect?"

His tone was bland and he lifted his brows, but Ali swore she saw a muscle tick along his jaw. The sight nearly made her grin. When they were kids that little spasm had served as a warning that the fuse to Luke's temper was burning shorter. What did he have to be angry about? The possibilities left her emboldened.

"My philosophy is if you're going to do something, you ought to do it well."

"I like your...philosophy. In fact, I wouldn't mind exploring it in more detail." Now his lips did bow. "Maybe I could learn something new."

She ignored the gooseflesh his statement had popping up on her skin. The evening air was chilly, that was all, and the wine had made her light-headed since she'd consumed it on an empty stomach. It wasn't the promise of passion that she saw in his gaze that was causing her body to tremble in anticipation.

She deliberately crossed her arms. "So, have you decided when you will be *leaving* Trillium?"

"No." He tilted his head to one side. "Is my staying for a little while longer a problem for you?"

She gave a careless shrug. "I have no problem with it. Stay as long as you like. I just figured someone as busy and important as you would have better things to do with his time than watch the grass grow in our little backwater."

Those were the very words he'd used once upon a time, but he didn't appear to remember the conversation.

"I've got nothing against Trillium."

Her arms dropped to her sides. "Since when? You couldn't leave fast enough eleven years ago. You were in such a hurry, you never even said goodbye."

"I told you I was leaving, Ali. You knew. We discussed it often enough."

"Discussed it? We didn't *discuss* anything."

"Right. We argued."

"What did you expect? You made your decision and that was the end of it as far as you were concerned. You were going. There was nothing left to do but pack the Harley's saddlebags. And you did. You packed up and you left—"

Me. She managed at least to keep that final word unspoken, holding on to some of her pride in the process. Even so, she felt exposed and appalled that she'd let all of this ancient history be unearthed.

"I had to go," he said quietly. "You remember how it was. I didn't have a future here. Everything seemed so predetermined. *Poor Luke Banning.* God, I was so tired of the pity and the way everyone just figured I'd end up facedown in a ditch someday like my old man had. I had to get away if I was going to make something of myself."

And he had. Ali couldn't argue with the results. But her tone was frosty when she reminded him, "So you said at the time."

"I never meant to hurt you." He took one hand out of his pocket and held it out, as if beseeching her to understand and to finally accept what he had done all those years before. "I'm sorry that I did."

That made it twice during the course of their conversation that he had apologized, although Ali didn't figure the first "sorry" counted since he hadn't been sure why he'd issued it in the first place. Either way, though, it didn't matter. She suddenly realized the words weren't important. His current contrition changed nothing. It didn't leave her feeling vindicated or superior. It just made her sad, because she could tell even now that if Luke Banning could rewind the years and do it all over again, he would still get on his Harley and go.

In fact, he wasn't back now. Not really. He was just on Trillium for a week, maybe two. Once his curiosity was satisfied and his back sufficiently patted by all of the locals who had once pitied him, Luke would be gone again. The Conlans's silent partner would return to New York where his high-rise apartment and high-profile life waited for him.

And Ali would be left behind. Again.

"I don't suppose I'll be getting that glass of wine," he said.

She shook her head slowly. "I doubt this vintage is up to your standards."

How appropriate, Ali thought, that Bonnie Raitt was now singing so somberly about not letting someone break her heart again.

"I'll say good night then."

Ali didn't say good night. She slipped into the house as he spoke, and just before pulling the sliding glass door completely closed, she told Luke goodbye.

* * *

Luke walked back up the beach in the sparse light of dusk. The temperature had dipped considerably once the sun set. He told himself that was why he felt so chilled. It had nothing to do with the cool way in which Ali had dismissed him. He hadn't missed the fact that she'd said goodbye rather than good night.

Going to see her had not been on his agenda this evening. It certainly was not why he'd begged off from dinner with Audra and Dane. He'd intended to poke around his grandmother's home, making a list of any necessary repairs. First thing in the morning he planned to call a local carpenter. He was determined to get the ball rolling before tourist season kicked off and the island was thick with people dreaming of a vacation home. His plan was to clear the cottage of his grandmother's personal effects, get the structure up to code and then stick a For Sale sign out front. But earlier this evening when he'd pulled his motorcycle to a stop next to the quaint bungalow, he'd heard music echoing through the trees. He hadn't been able to resist seeking out the source. He was paying for his impulsiveness now.

He climbed the steps to the cottage's rear porch and settled onto the swing, idly setting it into motion with one foot. The rhythmic squawk from the rusted chains that secured it to the porch ceiling competed with the tree frogs' high-pitched chorus, but Luke hardly noticed.

He was thinking about that damned kiss.

* * *

Morning was Ali's favorite time of the day. It always had been. When they were girls, Audra used to sleep till noon. Not Ali. She still woke before the birds began their dawn concert and long before the sun peeked over the tall trees to the east of the cottage. In the winter, she would sit in a rocking chair by the sliding glass door, sipping her first cup of coffee and watching the spreading light wink on the ice. Now that the weather had turned warmer, she pulled on a robe over her pajamas and took her coffee out on the deck.

This was her habit even when she was not due in to Saybrook's, and so she was comfortably reclining in one of the Adirondack chairs and halfway through her first cup of French roast when she heard a big splash followed by a lot of swearing.

She knew who was doing the swearing, and she knew what she *hoped* had caused the splash. Curiosity demanded she find out if she was right. So Ali scooted out of her seat and, coffee cup still in hand, walked down to the beach in her slippers. She followed the sand past an outcropping of trees to the neighboring property, and then sucked in a deep breath. Sure enough, Luke was standing on his grandmother's porch, sopping wet. She'd figured he'd somehow managed to fall in to the lake. But she hadn't considered that by the time she reached the property line he would have stripped off every last scrap of his drenched clothing. She looked away, but not before getting an eyeful. The man certainly had improved with age, and that was saying a lot.

Because that admission irked her, she called out, "Is that a tattoo?"

In her periphery vision, she saw him jump before he managed to secure the towel he'd been using around his waist.

"Why don't you come a little closer and you can decide for yourself?"

She ignored his challenge. "Water's a little chilly, hmm?"

"It's freezing," he agreed.

She did walk closer now, her slippers already damp from the dew that coated the weeds and grass that lined the slope. A few feet up the slope a dozen wooden stairs made the climb easier. Ali took the stairs only halfway.

"You know, the last of the ice just melted a couple weeks ago."

"That became abundantly clear as soon as I hit the water," he drawled.

She tilted her head to one side. "What are you doing out here so early?"

"I spent the night."

"In there?" she pointed to the cottage.

"Yes."

The very idea seemed impossible. Sure, the old Luke had known how to do without what many people would consider basic necessities, but this wealthy man had to be too soft to "rough it," especially when he had a nice suite back at the resort already paid for through the end of the week. She knew that because she'd called the front desk the night before and had someone check.

"But there's no electricity."

"Or running water," he inserted with a grin. "Which is why I was forced to improvise."

"Why not just go back to Saybrook's?"

He shrugged. "I didn't feel like driving back last night, and this morning I figured the lake would do. I forgot how damned cold it is. I was just planning to splash some water on my face, but then the dock collapsed and I fell in. The temperature took my breath away."

"And yet you still managed to curse a blue streak," she said dryly.

"Sorry. I didn't mean to disturb you." He motioned toward the cup she held and grinned engagingly. "That wouldn't happen to be for me, would it?"

Ali snorted. "In your dreams."

His demeanor changed then. Gone were the laughter and the casual attitude. Even with the space of a half-dozen wooden steps separating them, she saw the awareness sharpen his gaze. "You don't want to know what I dreamed about last night, Ali. Trust me."

"No, trust *me*," she stressed. "I have no interest in your dreams unless they have something to do with Saybrook's proposed golf course."

His posture relaxed a bit then. "Funny you should

mention that. I've been giving your idea more thought and I would like to go over the site today if you can spare a few hours to show me around."

A few hours with Luke Banning? Oh, no. She would let Audra or Dane handle that, Ali decided.

"Sorry. I'm not going in to the office today. In fact, I have the rest of the week off."

Luke wasn't deterred. "Good. Then I won't be taking you away from anything important," he replied.

"Of all the arrogant, self-centered..." She reeled in her temper, deciding the blistering diatribe she had in mind was a waste of good breath. Instead she said succinctly, "I have plans."

"What kind of plans?" he asked, running his hands through his hair. It stuck up at odd angles, which was the only reason, Ali told herself, that her fingers itched to smooth it down.

She cleared her throat. "The kind of plans that aren't any of your business."

He shrugged. "Well, when you find some time, come back over and get me."

"You'll be here?" she asked, unable to mask her surprise. A night in his boyhood home seemed almost inconceivable. Surely whatever soft sentiment had prompted him to stay last night had withered in the hard light of a new day.

But he was nodding. "All day. In fact, probably be spending the better part of the next several days here."

"And the nights?"

He grinned. "I'm not sure where I'll pass those. Yet."

"Why?"

"Just getting the place in order. Know a good local carpenter?"

Baffled, she replied, "Tom Whitey, of course."

On the island, pretty much everyone entrusted their home's upkeep to Tom, just as anyone who owned a boat visited the marina Tom's brother, Joe, owned. The Whitey family was as much of an island institution as Saybrook's.

A thought occurred to her then. "You're fixing up the place?"

Did that mean he intended to return to Trillium on a more regular basis? The little tremble she felt at the thought of having Luke next door for a few weeks each summer was borne of annoyance rather than interest, she assured herself.

"Some things will need to be updated before I can put the property on the market." One side of his mouth lifted. "I guess I'll have to add a new dock to the list now."

"You're selling."

He nodded, his gaze cutting away. "I'm thinking of dividing the parcel, too." He gestured toward the water and then over to where the woods again met the beach. "I've got enough lake frontage here for at least a couple of homes."

Ali dismissed the disappointment she felt. The man

was a businessman, an entrepreneur. He'd made a good portion of his fortune in real estate. Why should she have expected him to turn a blind eye to the profit potential here?

"It's a nice piece of property and the cottage has a lot of character even if it is on the small side," she agreed. "I'm sure you'll have no shortage of buyers. There's not much available on the sunset side of the island, nor is there much vacant lake frontage left on the mainland let alone on Trillium."

"You won't mind new neighbors?" he asked.

Ali shrugged, even though the thought of sharing her private haven with other people held little appeal. It was bad enough that campers and hikers often sauntered into her midst from the surrounding state land. If she had the money, which she certainly did not at this point with every last penny sunk into the resort, she would make him an offer herself.

"Whoever buys it probably won't stay year-round. I can tolerate anyone for a weekend or so," she said meaningfully.

And with that she turned and walked back down the steps.

"See you later," he hollered.

Ali waited until her slippers were touching sand to call back, "*Goodbye,* Luke."

Back in her cottage, she had barely managed to pour herself another cup of coffee when she turned to find

Luke on her deck, tapping insistently on the sliding glass door. He was still wearing one of his grandmother's floral print towels around his waist. In his hands were the dripping garments in which he had taken his impromptu swim.

"What do you want?" she asked through the screen, although she figured she knew.

"Do you think you could throw these in your dryer for me?" His lips, she noted, were tinted blue and goose bumps covered the taut muscles of his chest.

Once upon a time, Ali might have wished Luke Banning would die a slow and painful death, but she didn't want the man to expire from hypothermia while standing on her deck and ruin her perfectly good morning.

"Come in before you catch pneumonia," she said, sliding the screen open. Once he was inside, she peeled off the oversize navy robe she wore and handed it to him, exchanging it for the wet bundle he held. "Here. Put this on."

When he glanced at her curiously, she added, "It's the only thing of mine that's going to fit you."

"Thanks."

Luke nearly smiled as he shrugged into it. Ali was literally giving him the clothes off her back. He thanked God the robe was not some fluffy pink number, although even if it had been he still would have put it on. He'd never been so damned cold in all his life.

The soft fabric was warm from her body and it

smelled like her, a subtle vanilla scent that he remembered from long ago. She looked like he remembered, too, but not quite. Without the robe, he could see that she was wearing a thin-strapped tank top and drawstring lounging pants. Silk lingerie couldn't have been sexier or have done a better job of highlighting her small, firm breasts and long, tapered legs.

She crossed her arms over her chest, as if guessing the direction of his thoughts. "Do you want some coffee?"

"Please."

She walked back into the kitchen and he followed her, glancing around as she got a mug down and filled it.

"You've done a lot of work in here, I see."

Even that was an understatement. The room had been overhauled. Gone were the ruffled curtains and Formica countertops her grandmother had favored. It was now distinctly Ali with its terra-cotta-colored walls, rich granite countertops, maple cabinets and a no-nonsense Roman shade at the window over the sink. She'd always been one for clean lines and bold colors, and yet the place was definitely homey thanks to the framed botanical prints that hung on the wall next to the table. He had walk-in closets in his penthouse that were larger than the entire kitchen, but nothing about his modernly furnished apartment made him want to sigh.

He did now, though.

Luke blamed his sudden melancholy on the fact that he'd spent the night in his boyhood bed. Even with a decade's worth of dust coating the furniture in his room, he'd sworn he could smell the lemon wood polish Elsie Banning had used. God, how he missed her. He'd half expected to hear his grandmother banging around in the kitchen when he'd woke that morning, as wrapped in memories as he had been tangled in musty sheets. But no bacon had been sizzling on the stove. The small room had been dark and oppressively quiet. He'd opened the cottage's windows not so much to air out the interior as to bring in the sounds of nature. Anything to end that silence.

Of course, some nature had already found its way inside, he recalled now. And with a half grin he told Ali, "I think I have a family of raccoons in the attic. I heard something thumping around in the middle of the night."

"You also have skunks under the back porch," she replied, doing a lousy job of camouflaging her delight. "Or at least you did last summer. I nearly got sprayed when I was cutting down the weeds."

He snorted out a laugh. "Nice to know somebody has gotten some use out of the place while I've been gone." He finished off the coffee and pointed toward the machine on the counter behind her. "Do you mind?"

She moved out of the way. "Help yourself."

As he refilled the mug, he said quietly, "I'm going to have to clean it out."

"My coffeemaker?"

"No." He took a sip of his hot beverage, scalding his

tongue, but he knew that wasn't why his eyes stung. "The cottage. I'm going to have to clean it out."

"You can hire people for that."

"I need to do it." He pushed a hand through his hair, which was still damp. "I haven't been in my grandmother's room since she passed away. I closed the door the day she died and I never went back in. I need to go through her things."

"I can help, if you'd like."

He hadn't expected her to offer. Her expression told him neither had she. Was it obligation that had prompted her kindness? He wanted to believe it was something more.

"Thanks, Ali. I'd appreciate that."

"I miss her, too, you know. And my own Gran. They were good people, solid. You could depend on them." She laid a hand on his arm, squeezed, and he found himself immersed in an unexpected eddy of emotions.

"Ali, I—"

But she was letting go of his arm and moving away.

"I'm going to get dressed. If you're hungry, there's milk in the fridge and cereal in the pantry. Bowls are in the same cupboard they always were. Help yourself."

Good, solid, dependable. Ali was those things as well. But as he watched her disappear down the short hallway off the kitchen, Luke knew that it wasn't only those attributes that had his stomach coiling into knots.

CHAPTER FOUR

ALI stood in her bedroom, staring sightlessly at the contents of the bureau drawer she'd pulled open. She was more than a little unnerved by Luke's show of emotions. Even when they were dating he had played his feelings close to the vest. In her kitchen, however, for a brief time, his grief had been visible, damned near palpable, wafting off him like heat from asphalt in August. Even at Elsie's funeral, he'd remained stoic, pushing Ali away when she'd tried to get close. Now, he hadn't needed to push. Ali had distanced herself all on her own.

His arrogance the night before had made it easy for her to turn away. His need now made it all but impossible for her not to want to offer comfort, which she supposed was why she was in her room, staring at the neatly folded clothes that she had arranged by color, and wondering just what in the hell had possessed her to offer to help him clear out his grandmother's belongings.

Blowing out a breath, she extracted a pair of shorts

and a plain cotton T-shirt. She would go for a run, letting the crisp air clear her head of these thoughts and this newly resurrected need.

When she stepped back out into the living room, Luke was sitting in her favorite chair near the window, an empty cereal bowl on the table next to him and a fresh cup of coffee in his hands, judging from the steam curling over the lip.

He didn't look at her when he said, "It's easy to believe the rest of the world doesn't exist when you sit here and stare out at the lake." He laughed then. "Hell, it's easy to believe Wisconsin doesn't exist."

She'd had exactly that same thought from time to time, even though Green Bay was only about a hundred miles to the west.

"They say seeing is believing."

He did turn now. "Going out for some exercise?"

"Yes."

"I run, too."

"Really?" That surprised her. Ali had averaged twenty-five miles a week since her junior year in high school, but Luke had never been one to pull on a pair of Nikes and join her.

"Took it up in New York," he said on a shrug. "It's easy to fall into an unhealthy lifestyle there when you work long hours and eat out."

"Amazingly we have the same pitfalls here," she said dryly.

His smile was slightly sheepish. "I guess so."

"I'll be back in about an hour," she said, kneeling down to tie her shoes. "I'm sure your clothes will be dry before then."

One of his eyebrows rose. "Eager to be rid of me, I see. Should I lock up when I leave?"

Ali sighed, the gulf between them seeming to widen once more. "This is Trillium, Luke. Only the seasonal residents flip their dead bolts."

He frowned. "You should, too, you know, especially being out here on your own and surrounded by state land where anyone is welcome to tramp on through."

She tilted her head to one side. "Don't you think I can take care of myself?"

"I'd rather not find out. Bad things can happen any-where, Ali."

She tried to be put out by his misplaced concern and yet she couldn't help but feel oddly touched.

"I do lock up at night," she admitted. "Satisfied?"

That one word seemed to hang in the air between them. The three innocuous syllables took on a whole new meaning when Luke's gaze strayed to her lips.

It was a long moment before he said, "I guess that's better than nothing." Then he stood. "Mind if I take a shower while you're gone?"

"Help yourself."

Once outside, Ali ran as if the hounds of hell were chasing her and she paid for it. She had a nasty stitch in her side after the first mile that made even a brisk walk painful. Still, she pressed on, giving Luke time to take his shower, dress in his dry clothes and clear out of her cottage.

When she arrived home he was gone, but that didn't save her from thinking about him. Little reminders were everywhere. His bowl and spoon were on the counter next to his coffee mug. She rinsed them and put them in the dishwasher. Then she cleaned out the coffeepot and tossed out the grounds, trying to eradicate every reminder of his presence. She almost managed it in the kitchen, but the bathroom was another story. A second plush blue towel hung beside hers on the bar next to the old-fashioned claw-foot tub.

She tugged off her sweaty clothes and turned on the shower. Stepping under the spray it occurred to her that she didn't see a washcloth anywhere. Reaching for the soap, she pictured rather vividly Luke working that very same bar into a thick lather while he stood naked in the same spot. Disgusted with herself, she turned the spray to cold. The jerk was back a matter of days and already he had her fantasizing.

By midmorning she had rearranged the furniture in her cozy living room, packed away her winter clothes and swept the deck. She planned to wash the windows on the side of the cottage that faced the lake. She was a worker, not a lounger, which is why even with a coveted few days off from her job, she was determined to be productive and make the most of her time. Her parents often chided her for being too busy.

"You need to take some time for yourself," was a familiar refrain whenever she spoke with them on the telephone.

Time to do what? Manicure her nails or goop some green gunk on her cheeks for a facial? That was what Audra would do, but Ali had never seen the point in such pampering. Or at least that's what she'd told herself. She glanced down at her hands. They were roughened from work, the nails filed to a short and practical length. Just the night before those fingers had gripped Luke's broad shoulders, the blunt tips sinking into firm muscle as she'd held on.

She let out a sigh and went in search of a ladder.

Luke was sitting in one of the Adirondack chairs on her deck when she returned. For a man who'd once walked out of her life with such apparent ease, she was having a hard time getting rid of him now.

"And he's back again," she muttered.

Luke grinned. "Your hospitality makes it hard to stay away."

"What do you want now?"

"There's a loaded question," he said. When she scowled, he turned serious. "I thought we could go over the property if you've got the time. Weather is perfect for a hike and I'd really like a firsthand look."

"I told you I'm on vacation this week."

He inclined his head toward the ladder. "A working vacation?"

"So? I've never been one for sitting around."

"Well, if it's a working vacation, then you won't mind taking a walk with me in the name of business."

She opened her mouth to refuse, but then changed her mind. He was bound to continue pestering her.

Sighing heavily, she replied, "Let's get this over with."

Fifteen minutes later, she had donned a pair of hiking boots and stood next to her car waiting for Luke to walk over. Instead he rumbled up her drive on the Harley.

She eyed the bike tucked between his denim-clad legs and said, "You're not expecting me to get on that thing, are you?"

The words came out sharp because part of her wanted to. Part of her wanted to be reckless and throw all caution to the wind for a change.

"Come on, Ali," he coaxed seductively. "It will be like old times."

His promise had heat curling through her system, which she fought to ignore. And the part of her that remained firmly planted in the practical, said, "We can take my car."

"Where's your sense of adventure?"

"It left town about the same time you did," she replied, raising one eyebrow for emphasis.

But Luke only grinned. "Come on, *Alice*. Live a little."

"Don't call me Alice."

He merely revved the bike's engine, well aware that she detested the use of her full name.

"I'll get on if you'll agree to wear a helmet," she told him at last.

She figured she had him there, but Luke reached behind him and grabbed the one that was strapped onto the back of the black leather seat.

He started to put it on, but then stopped and smiled. "Of course, if I wear it, then you won't have one. Are you sure you want me to have it?"

She wrenched it from his hands and put it on, muttering curses as she secured the strap under her chin. Then she hiked a leg over the seat and settled in behind him.

She planned to hold on to the back of the seat, angled as far away from his body as she could manage. But then he shot off down the bumpy road and her good intentions were left in the dust. Ali would have been left in the dust as well if she had not snagged a handful of Luke's T-shirt. She fisted the fabric in her fingers before the wind could plaster it against his taut abdomen, and then gave up completely. She wrapped her arms around him and leaned in. She was flush against his back from her shoulders to the V of her thighs, and the humming sensation she felt had nothing to do with the motorcycle's vibration as it skimmed over the rutted road.

Fifteen minutes of delicious torture later, they arrived

at Saybrook's. She hopped off the Harley as soon as it
came to a stop, needing distance but wanting something
else entirely.

"I thought we were going to walk over the property?" she said.

"I wanted to grab some fresh clothes first." He wrin-
kled his nose. "These smell like lake water."

And here she'd thought they'd smelled like him.

"I won't be long. You can wait in my suite if you'd
like." The smile that accompanied his suggestion had
her shaking her head.

"I'll wait down here, thanks." As she tried to work
the helmet's chin strap free, she said, "You still drive
like an idiot."

He stepped in front of her, and just as he had done a
hundred times when they were younger, he pushed her
hands away, unhooked the strap and pulled off the
helmet. Her hair tumbled free. She had scooped it all up
inside before leaving the cottage. The move was practical. The wind would have tangled it into painful knots.
Luke set the helmet on the bike's seat now and reached
out to comb his fingers through it, holding on to the ends
and using them to draw her closer.

"You always had the softest hair," he said, his tone
so low she almost thought she had imagined the words.

A car pulled into the parking lot then, intruding on
the moment and saving Ali from having to speak. As
Luke's hands fell away from her hair, she wondered

what she would have said in response to his intimate observation anyway.

She managed to walk into the resort on liquid limbs, eager to barricade herself behind the safety of her desk until she got a grip on her pulse. Of course, Audra was in the lobby when Ali and Luke entered. Her twin waved to Luke as he headed toward the elevator and fell into step beside Ali.

"Out for a joy ride with Luke?"

"Not a joy ride. It's business," she said, proud that she sounded so blasé when her pulse was still zipping along in overdrive and her skin felt as hot as the Harley's exhaust pipe. "Luke and I are going to walk over the golf course site."

"What are you doing here, then?" Audra asked.

"He needed a change of clothes."

She wanted to kick herself as soon as the words were spoken.

Audra, of course, was grinning broadly. "A change of clothes, hmm? Does that mean he didn't come back to the resort last night?"

They reached the management offices and Ali entered her well ordered one without bothering to reply. Audra, of course, turned in as well, closing the door behind her.

"I wonder where Luke could have slept?" she mused aloud, eyebrows arching.

"At his grandmother's cottage," Ali replied primly. "Get your mind out of the gutter."

Ali sat at her desk and booted up her computer to check her e-mail, hoping her sister would take the hint and go away. No such luck, of course. Audra settled one hip on the corner of the desk—no easy task in her snug little skirt—and picked up a paperweight.

"Interesting," Audra said, idly rolling the weight from one palm to the other. "Luke chose to sleep in a dusty, musty cottage that has no running water or electricity, food or coffee, rather than return to his nice, comfortable suite of rooms at the resort. I wonder what could have compelled him to stay there?"

"Maybe it was the view of Lake Michigan. Maybe he was feeling sentimental. I didn't ask," Ali snapped, jabbing at the keyboard to enter her password.

"I could hazard a guess."

Ali stopped typing. "Don't, Audra."

"Don't what?"

"Don't make this into more than it is."

"Define 'this,'" Audra said, not put off in the least by Ali's cool tone. "Did something happen between the two of you last night?"

"No. Of course not." But she was pretty sure she was blushing. "I mean, we kissed. It was nothing."

"Nothing? Okay, Al. If you say so."

"I say so!" she shouted, slapping her palms onto the desk top. "I'm no longer the girl who worshipped the ground he walked on."

Audra frowned then. "I don't seem to remember it

ever being that one-sided, sweetie. He worshipped you plenty right back."

"But…" *He still left.* She shook off the bitter memories. "Look, it doesn't matter. That's ancient history. Luke is here on business. Neither one of us is interested in taking a stroll down memory lane."

"I don't know about that." Audra pursed her lips thoughtfully before continuing. "He looked plenty interested just now when he was helping you get that helmet off."

"Were you spying on us?"

"Please, I don't spy. Much. I was in the lobby. I heard the motorcycle and I was curious if it was Luke's since I didn't see his bike in the lot this morning when I arrived for work. So, I did what any normal curious person would do. I looked out the window that faces the lot."

Audra grinned now. "And I've got to tell you, Al. I was a little surprised to see you on the back of his Harley with your arms wrapped around him like you never planned to let go."

"I was merely trying to keep from falling off. He still drives like he's racing against the devil."

Audra made a little humming sound that set Ali's teeth on edge.

"Whatever you say."

"Don't you have work to do?"

"Actually I'm on my way to meet Seth for lunch." A

smile bloomed on Audra's face as she stood. "At home. It's going to be a long lunch. A *very long* lunch."

Ali rolled her eyes. "I don't want to hear about it," she muttered. "I *don't* want to hear about it."

At Ali's insistence, they left Luke's motorcycle in the lot at Saybrook's and walked out past the cottages to the adjoining land. Much of the acreage was dense forest, populated with hardwoods and cedars that left the air fragrant. Dried leaves and decaying wood crunched under their feet, and as he and Ali picked their way through the newly sprouted ferns, they surprised a couple of whitetail deer.

The sights, the sounds, even the smell had Luke feeling nostalgic. In New York he'd told himself he hadn't missed this kind of nature. He'd told himself Central Park was enough green space and wildlife for him. But now he was inhaling deeply, glad to be back. Maybe he should consider holding on to his grandmother's place. After all, he would be returning to Trillium occasionally now that he had business here.

His gaze strayed to Ali. Soft light sprinkled down through the newly budded leaves to play over her face. What would her reaction be if he told her he was thinking of coming back a few times a year?

"Why are you looking at me that way?" she asked sharply and he realized he'd been staring.

"There's a spiderweb caught in your hair," he replied.

The socialites he knew back in New York would have screamed with unholy abandon at such a statement. Ali merely ran a hand over her head and then pointed toward a thick growth of trees.

"There's a little stream just beyond those trees, I think. It runs nearly dry by late summer, but it might make a decent hazard."

Business. That's what her mind was on. Luke decided it should be on his as well.

"It isn't going to be cheap to clear this," he said, glancing up at the towering trees.

"No, I don't suppose it will. But I like the idea of keeping it as natural as possible. I'd like to see the fairways just wide enough to make play enjoyable without turning this into a meadow." She smiled then and his breath caught at the joy and excitement crowding her expression. "It's going to be incredible."

"Incredible," he repeated softly, and then flushed when she turned to look at him. "Which reminds me, we need to come up with a name for the course."

"Actually I've given that some thought." She plucked a leaf off a nearby bush, looking somewhat uncertain now.

"And?"

"I was thinking we could call it The Rebel."

"Named for anyone you know?" he asked wryly.

Half of her mouth crooked up into a grin. "A couple of people, actually."

"Oh? And what does Audra think of it?"

"I haven't asked her yet. I figured I'd run it by you first."

He snorted out a laugh. "It suits."

Rebel. He certainly had been one. So had Audra. Odd that they were both back now when they had once been equally eager to go. Of course, he wouldn't be staying for long.

They walked until they came to a gravel road that led back to the resort. It was a private road, but a car was pulled onto the shoulder, its front end half buried in the ferns.

"Nice car," Luke commented. "I didn't think many islanders went for foreign numbers."

"They don't."

"A guest then?"

"Maybe." But Ali was frowning.

As they made their way back to the resort she wondered what Bradley Townsend's Mercedes had been doing parked there.

CHAPTER FIVE

BEFORE noon the next day, Ali had managed to wash half of the cottage's windows. Normally she would have flipped on her stereo to perform such a boring chore, but there'd been no need. From just over the rise came the steady thump of bass and the wail of electric guitar.

Luke had arrived early that morning. She'd heard his motorcycle revving up the lane as she'd waited for the coffeemaker to finish its task. Not long after that she'd spotted Tom Whitey's pickup truck idling past as well. Apparently Luke was making good on his plan to see to some repairs before putting the place up for sale.

As she washed the window, Bruce Springsteen belted out "Born in the U.S.A." and Ali mentally shook her head. Luke always had enjoyed his music loud and a little gritty. The Boss was his favorite singer, but another performer came in a close second. She figured she was probably the only person on the planet who knew Luke had a thing for Frank Sinatra.

She'd teased him mercilessly when she'd stopped over at his grandmother's one afternoon back when they were teenagers and discovered his fondness. Bad-boy Luke Banning crooning tunes from the 1950s. What would his friends say? He'd been nineteen at the time, all cocky attitude and lean muscle. She'd been sixteen and, as she recalled, incredibly curious about the odd sizzle that had shimmied up her spine when he'd plucked her off her feet and carried her down to the lake.

He'd tossed her in from the end of the same dock that had disintegrated beneath his feet the previous morning. But back then, he had stood at the end of it, laughing uproariously when her head had bobbed out of the water. His laughter had stopped abruptly, however, when she'd slogged toward shore, white T-shirt and shorts plastered to her skin. By fourteen, Audra had been filling out a C-cup bra and had already had high school boys drooling. At sixteen, Ali's proportions had remained much less conspicuous. But she still remembered the way Luke's eyes had widened and then his gaze had cut away. A flush had crept up his neck to his cheeks before he'd made excuses and stormed back up to the house. Ali had known with all the certainty of a girl falling in love for the first time, that there would never be anyone for her but Luke.

"Thinking of me?"

She snapped out of the past, so startled to hear his

voice that she nearly fell off her perch on the stepladder she'd positioned against the side of the cottage.

"God! Don't sneak up on a person that way," she snarled, more irritated by the memory than by his present intrusion. She set aside the wad of paper towels and the spray bottle of cleaner, and climbed down. Her tone was only marginally more civil when she asked, "What do you want?"

"Tom decided to call it a day. He got a nasty splinter helping me drag the old dock out of the lake. I was wondering if you'd be interested in grabbing some lunch?" He smiled. "My treat."

"I'm really—"

"Busy?" One eyebrow lifted as he glanced toward the ladder. "Won't that keep?"

"I want to finish this today."

"But you'll stop for food at some point, right? Why not have lunch with me? Consider it a payback for breakfast yesterday." He winked then. "Besides, I'm curious about some things Tom mentioned."

Ali knew she was being baited. Cursing herself, she bit anyway. "What *things?*"

He shrugged. "Just some island gossip about your developer boyfriend."

"You asked Tom Whitey about Bradley Townsend?" Her tone was incredulous and a couple of decibels louder than it had been. "What gives you the right to go poking around in my private life?"

"I didn't go poking around. Tom brought it up." His easygoing smile had her gritting her teeth. "You know how news travels on the island."

Didn't she just. Now she was curious as well.

"Give me half an hour."

Thirty minutes later, Ali had showered and changed into a pair of neatly pressed khaki trousers and a lightweight argyle sweater in hues of navy and green. Surveying her appearance in the bedroom mirror, she thought she looked ready either to tee one up on the first hole of a golf course or head to class at a private girls' academy. Sometimes, she wished she could be more inspired in her clothing choices, but the truth was, she liked the clean lines of the classics. They suited her personality— most of the time. Every so often, though, she felt a little unconventional, a little eager to shake up the status quo.

Like now, she decided as Luke pulled up on his motorcycle. She could tell from the gleam in his eye that he expected her to argue. She didn't. She strapped on the helmet, swung a leg over the seat and, telling herself it was purely in the interest of safety, she wrapped her arms around him and held on tight.

By the time they pulled into the Sandpiper's parking lot, though, she was regretting her spontaneity. The last thing she needed was to set more tongues wagging. It was a moot point she realized when Joel Norville walked out of the restaurant, followed by his wife, Courtney.

Luke and the Conlans had gone to school with both of them. Courtney had been Courtney Lords back then, a varsity cheerleader known as much for her vicious gossiping as her ability to do the splits. She was still a vicious gossip.

It was small of Ali to think it now, but she couldn't help but feel that the other woman had "peaked" in high school. Other than her marriage to Joel just after commencement, five months after which the first of three little Norvilles had been born, she'd done precious little else that could be considered productive. As for Joel, if not for his father's plumbing supply business on the mainland, he would have had a difficult time finding employment. Ali had never met a lazier pair. Ironically, back at Trillium High, Courtney and Joel had taken sadistic delight in tormenting Luke about his lack of parents and dearth of privileges.

Now they were grinning as if they had been appointed to head up the welcoming committee.

"Luke Banning!" Courtney shouted.

"Hey, good to see you, man," Joel enthused.

"Hello, Courtney. Joel."

Luke shook their hands, nodding politely.

"Is that a real Rolex?" Joel had the audacity to ask, turning Luke's wrist for a better view.

One side of Luke's mouth quirked up. "Nah. I bought it on a street corner in New York. Twenty bucks. Looks authentic, though, huh?"

Ali had a hard time hiding her grin as the other man frowned in confusion.

"Hi, Ali," Courtney said, as if just now noticing her presence.

"Hello." Manners dictated that she ask, "How are your kids?"

Courtney snorted. "Oh, driving me up one wall, across the ceiling and down the other side. But I love them. I'm glad I had them so young. I've heard that women in their thirties often have a hard time conceiving. Speaking of that, is Audra having any luck?"

Ali felt her mouth fall open before she managed to say, "I wouldn't presume to ask her."

The subtle reprimand was lost on the other woman.

"You know," Courtney went on, putting her hands on her full hips and discreetly sucking in her stomach. "I've also heard women who give birth later in life have a harder time getting their figures back."

"It didn't seem to be a problem for my mother," Ali replied tightly. "Even after twins."

"Well, Audra shouldn't wait too long. Her eggs aren't getting any younger." Courtney smiled cattily. "Of course, as her twin, you know that."

Ali was still trying to work up a scathing reply when Courtney turned her attention back to Luke. Apparently satisfied that she had pointed out the advancing age of Ali's reproductive tract, she said, "You're as good-looking as ever, Luke. It seems to me that I read in a magazine a couple months back that you were all but engaged. Still heading toward the altar?"

"You shouldn't believe everything you read in the tabloids," he admonished. "Most of it is fiction."

Her eyes lit up like a child's at Christmas. "Good. I have a cousin who is just dying to meet you."

"I won't be around long enough to socialize."

"That's not what the grapevine is saying," Courtney said. "We hear you're looking to invest, possibly in the resort. Everybody on the island is talking about you. Your ears must be burning," Courtney added, her grin somehow managing to be sly and lascivious at the same time.

"It's just like old times then," Luke replied. The sarcasm in his tone wrung nervous laughter from the other couple.

"If you'll excuse us, we were just going in for lunch," Ali said.

"Is that just like old times, too?" Courtney asked. Before Ali could respond, the other woman added, "Oh, no. That's right. I heard you were seeing someone these days. A mainlander, I believe."

"Come on, Courtney. I need to get back to work," Joel said. Hitching up his pants, he said importantly, "I'm the co-owner in my father's business these days. I'm helping out with a job on the north shore today. A lot of big new homes have gone in there during the past several years. It's been very good for business."

"I'll bet," Luke replied.

"I ran into Tom Whitey at the post office this morning and he said he was stopping at your old place to give you a quote on repairs. If you need any plumbing supplies, be sure to let me know."

"I'll do that."

Finally they were gone, but Ali should have guessed the Norvilles wouldn't be the only ones to sidle up to Luke. By the time they had settled into a booth at the rear of the Sandpiper, half a dozen more islanders had welcomed Luke home.

Even Sheriff Curt Dolan came by to shake his hand, acting as if back when he'd been a deputy he hadn't ticketed Luke half a dozen times for speeding and threatened to toss him in jail over a little tussle that broke out at the marina. The other kids involved had been let off with a stern warning, but Deputy Dolan had cuffed Luke, put him in the back of his squad car and driven him to the police station, making him sweat it out for a good hour before releasing him to his grandmother's custody.

Now, as the older man fingered the bill of his official-issue hat, he said, "I always knew you'd wind up a big shot."

"I thought you figured me for winding up in the *big house*," Luke countered smoothly, and Ali kicked him under the table.

The sheriff cleared his throat as heat crept up his cheeks. Before he turned to leave, he added meaningfully, "By the way, it's still illegal to ride that bike without a helmet. Fine's pretty stiff, too, but then I'd imagine you have the money to pay it these days."

"That I do."

After he walked away, Ali said, "Did you have to antagonize the man? He's the sheriff now."

"Sheriff? That figures," Luke scoffed. "Still, what's he going to do?"

"Maybe he'll arrest you for arrogance."

Luke laughed outright, causing heads to turn at the neighboring tables. He lowered his voice when he replied, "Believe me, Dolan wanted to a couple of times."

"He never liked you," Ali agreed.

Luke's lighthearted mood seemed to evaporate. He fiddled with a couple of packets of sugar from the center of the table and admitted, "I once heard him tell my grandmother that if she didn't get me under control we would both wind up in court: Me in leg irons and him testifying for the prosecution."

"Does that still bother you?" Ali asked quietly.

"Nah. I'm long over it." But even as he said it his fingers tensed on the little white packets until they burst and sugar granules scattered across the tabletop.

He glanced at her afterward, as if daring her to comment. She picked up a plastic-coated menu instead. After a few moments of studying it, she said, "It must feel good to have so many people eating crow."

"I didn't realize they served that at the Sandpiper,"

Luke replied, glancing at his own menu. "I wonder if it tastes like chicken."

The waitress came by then and took their orders and Ali steered the conversation to safer topics like the weather. Luke listened with only half an ear as she told him about lake level predictions and what the higher gas prices were likely to mean for the upcoming tourist season.

As she spoke, he was thinking instead about folks eating crow. Despite his flippant reply to Ali's question, he did indeed have strong feelings about his return. He liked the respect he saw, even the awe in the expressions of the islanders. Those things sure went down smoother than the pity and disgust he'd been treated to as child. In his teen years, he could admit he'd deserved some scorn. He'd fed right into their stereotype, the bad-ass biker flying down the highway a couple dozen miles over the posted speed limit.

Only a few people had seen something more in him than attitude and rebellion. He glanced across the table. Ali had been one of those people. It was one of the reasons he'd fallen in love with her.

He realized he was staring when she shifted uncomfortably in her seat.

"I believe you were going to tell me about a rumor you heard concerning Bradley," she said.

Bradley. Luke felt a muscle tick in his jaw. Even the man's name sounded like 24-karat gold, and despite all the wealth Luke had accumulated over the past decade, he still sometimes felt like he would never be more than silver plate.

He wasn't given to snap judgments, especially since he'd been on the receiving end one too many times over the years. But Tom Whitey's words of that morning seemed all the reason he needed to think poorly of the man Ali was seeing.

The waitress returned with their orders, burger and fries for Ali and lightly battered lake perch for him with a side order of the Sandpiper's signature cole slaw. God, he'd missed the stuff living in Manhattan.

"Well?" Ali prompted.

"Not a rumor. Tom just mentioned that the guy's reputation as a developer leaves a lot to be desired. He's not exactly environmentally friendly."

He reached over to snag a French fry from her plate. It was an old habit, even though it was something he hadn't done in too many years to count. He couldn't imagine what some of the high-class women he'd dated would say if he'd snatched food from their plates. Of course, fries weren't on the menu at any of the nouvelle cuisine establishments he dined in these days.

Ali frowned and swatted away his hand. "Are you accusing him of illegal activity? The state has plenty of regulations in place regarding development, especially on the Great Lakes."

"I'm not accusing the guy of doing anything illegal, and I don't think Tom was, either. But you and I both know that people can adhere to the letter of the law while skirting the spirit of it." He took a sip of his cola. "I'd just hate to see him get his foot in the door on Trillium."

She waved a hand dismissively. "Bradley's not interested in the island."

"I'd lay odds that he's interested, Ali. He put in a bid on the resort when it went on the market."

"He did not."

"That's what I heard."

"From who? Tom Whitey?"

He shrugged, not willing to admit that after his conversation with the contractor he'd placed a few calls. The information was easy enough to confirm, but he doubted Ali would appreciate his digging.

"You, Dane and Audra bought the resort for a song partly because the previous owners wanted it to stay with islanders. Nostalgia aside, anyone on the outside can smell the profit potential here."

She shook her head. "God, you're a piece of work. So, the only reason Bradley is dating me is to get in at Saybrook's? Is it so hard for you to believe that a handsome and wealthy man could be interested in *me?*"

He sensed the hurt behind her crisp words and he regretted it. "No, Ali. Of course not. I'm just…giving you a heads-up. A warning. That's all."

"People used to warn me about you," she reminded him with an arch of her brows.

"Yes, they did. And you didn't listen."

"Apparently I should have."

He lifted one side of his mouth into a smile. "Maybe you should have," he agreed. "But I'm glad you didn't."

He saw her draw in a breath, as if contemplating his words. But when she spoke, she returned to the subject they'd been discussing before their detour into boggy personal territory.

"Well, for your information, Bradley is concentrating his efforts on the mainland south of Petoskey. He has a waterfront condo development going in there. He doesn't have any plans for development on the island."

"Are you sure?"

She hesitated a moment, but then said, "Yes. I'm sure."

"Well someone is sniffing around. Tom has a friend at the county registrar's office and he said someone's been making inquiries about the tract of land we're after. We still don't have a purchase agreement hammered out. It could be that someone wants to beat us to the punch, and then maybe they could turn around and sell us the property at a hefty markup."

She leaned back in her seat and crossed her arms. "That someone is not Bradley."

The confident way in which she spoke the other man's name rankled for some reason.

Luke snagged another fry from her plate, dipping it in the little pile of ketchup she'd poured. Before popping it into his mouth, he asked, "You sound pretty sure of that. It makes me wonder how serious things are between the two of you."

"That's none of your business."

She was right. It was none of his business. He had no right to ask her anything personal. No right at all even though she had kissed him back rather enthusiastically the night before. He heard himself ask, "Does that mean you're not sleeping together?"

"God, you have nerve!"

"I'm just curious, because Tom said you'd only gone out on a date or two. I didn't figure you'd had a chance to—"

A French fry bounced off his nose, which he supposed was better than the slap he deserved. Why was he baiting her this way? Why was he asking questions that had answers he didn't want to know?

Ali stood. "I think lunch is over."

She was out the door before he could pull enough bills from his wallet to cover their meal, but Luke didn't figure she would get far on foot. He left his bike in the lot and set out after her, jogging along the shoulder of the road that led back toward the ferry dock and the island's main crossroads.

"Ali, wait!" he called.

She marched ahead. "Go away, Luke. I'm in no mood to talk to you."

When he was just behind her, he grabbed her elbow

and spun her around. He swore he felt scorched by the fury blazing in her eyes.

"I'm sorry, okay? I had no right to say that."

"No right," she agreed, voice shaking with anger. "No right at all."

"I'm sorry," he said again. "Come back to the restaurant. Let me give you a ride home or to Saybrook's."

She merely shook her head.

"Ali, please." He tried again. "I can't leave you here like this."

"Why?" she countered.

"Ali."

But she shook her head and then walked backward a few steps, putting more than physical distance between the pair of them. She no longer looked angry. Now she just appeared sad, resigned.

"Go, Luke. Leave. Don't you get it? I'm fine without you."

CHAPTER SIX

LUKE was in a foul mood by the time he returned to the resort. He'd taken a long ride on his Harley, berating himself the entire way. Why couldn't he leave Ali the hell alone? What did it matter whom she was seeing? Whom she slept with? The past was just that. He'd moved on. Surely she was entitled to do the same. And yet the thought of her making love with anyone else had acid scorching the lining of his stomach.

The last person he wanted to run into when he walked through Saybrook's refurbished lobby was Dane Conlan, but Ali's brother spotted him the moment he cleared the main entrance, almost as if Dane had been waiting for Luke to arrive.

"What the hell is going on?" Dane snarled.

He didn't bother with any pleasantries as he blocked Luke's path to the old-fashioned elevators.

Oh, yeah. He'd been waiting all right, Luke decided.

Irritation and anger burned bright in Dane's usually

easygoing gaze. He and Luke were about the same size, although Luke had a couple of inches in height on him. But the tight clench of Dane's jaw made him seem larger, more menacing at the moment. And it caused a bit of déjà vu, reeling time backward for both of them. They'd had more than a couple of arguments where Ali was concerned, and Luke would bet his last dollar that she was the reason behind her brother's irate expression.

Luke ran his tongue over his teeth. "I take it you talked to your sister."

"Yeah, I talked to her. She called me from Julie's floral shop near the Sandpiper about an hour ago. She needed a ride home after having lunch with you and she was plenty ticked off. What the hell is going on?" Dane demanded a second time.

"We had a disagreement."

"Jeez, Banning, you haven't even been back on the island a week. What in the hell could you and Ali have to fight over?"

The question seemed to hold a challenge, which Luke chose to ignore. He wasn't feeling up to exploring the answer at the moment.

"Nothing," he replied. "It was stupid and my fault." He tucked his hands into the front pockets of his jeans. But then he couldn't stop himself from asking, "What do you think of Townsend?"

Dane's brows tugged together in a frown. "What does Bradley Townsend have to do with this?"

When Luke remained silent, Dane's tight expression bloomed into a grin. "Ah. So, that was the source of the argument. You're not jealous, are you?"

"No," Luke scoffed. The very notion was absurd, he told himself, even as the hands in his pockets balled into tight fists. "I just…don't like the guy, that's all."

Even to his own ears, his announcement seemed rash. He hadn't *met* Bradley Townsend. He'd never so much as laid eyes on him. He had only the flimsiest of evidence to suggest the man was up to no good. In fact, he had no evidence, just the suspicion of a local carpenter and the tightness in his own gut, which could hardly be considered reliable at this point.

What's more, Townsend's relationship with Ali, was, as she'd so succinctly informed Luke that afternoon, none of his damned business.

Still, it gratified him immensely when Dane muttered, "Join the club."

"So, you don't like him, either?"

Dane cleared his throat, loyalty apparently kicking in to do damage control. "What I think of him doesn't matter," he qualified.

For some reason, the diplomatic reply left Luke feeling on firmer footing.

"Don't give me that BS, Conlan. He's dating your baby sister. As I recall, after you found out I'd kissed her you hauled me up by the shirtfront and threatened to kick my butt—which was highly doubtful, by the way."

"She was a kid at the time."

"She was seventeen."

"She was a kid," Dane repeated. "But she's an adult now. She knows her own mind."

"And you have no problem with this guy she's seeing? This Bradley Townsend?"

"I didn't say I have no problem with him," Dane admitted, but before Luke could feel too smug, the other man added, "I said it's none of my business."

Deciding to drop the matter for now, Luke said, "Well, I know something that is."

He then told Dane the concerns Tom Whitey had shared with him about Townsend's character and the fact that someone was sniffing around about the property they were preparing to buy.

Dane frowned. "That's not good. We're still in negotiations over a purchase price. I got a call this morning from the owner. I'm assuming he got wind of your return to town and our meeting and so now the price of the property has gone up. He claims to have another offer."

Luke ran a hand around the back of his neck, massaging the knotted muscles there. "I was afraid that might happen. We'd better get something in writing fast, then. Have you made a counteroffer?"

"I was waiting to discuss it with you."

"I think we need to give him what he's asking and get this thing sewed up quickly. Without that chunk of land Saybrook's can say goodbye to expansion. There's not another parcel that size bounding the resort."

"You think Townsend has anything to do with this?" Dane asked.

Luke shrugged. "He's a developer. I would be interested if I were him, even if only to buy it first and sell it to us for a higher price later. Ali doesn't seem to think he's got his eye on Trillium, though. She was pretty ticked off at me for even suggesting he might have something up his sleeve."

"Was that all you argued over?"

Luke felt a flush creep up his cheeks. "Not exactly."

Dane's gaze turned cool again. "Don't mess with her, Luke. Don't come back here and muck up her life when you don't plan to stay for long."

For some reason, Luke felt the need to point out: "You just said Ali's an adult. You said she knows her own mind."

"Yeah, well I'm making an exception where you're concerned. Consider yourself warned."

Luke nodded and his gut twisted. They had been best friends a dozen years ago, but even then Luke had always harbored a secret worry that Dane felt Luke wasn't good enough for his sister. Now, even though Luke was a multimillionaire, apparently he still wasn't.

Ali didn't see Luke for the next couple of days. She'd expected to run into him over the weekend, especially since she'd heard his motorcycle rev past on more than a couple of occasions, but he didn't drop in and she made a point of steering clear of him as well.

She went on her date with Bradley on Saturday, determined to have a good time, determined to ignore Luke's suspicions even after Bradley denied being on Trillium when she'd casually asked if he'd been at the resort earlier in the week. When he dropped her off at home afterward, Ali told herself the reason she didn't invite him in for a drink was because it was late and she was tired. It had nothing to do with Luke Banning and the old feelings he had bubbling to the surface.

On Monday she returned to work, hardly rested despite her time off. She was back in one of her old straight skirts, although she'd hemmed it a good three inches the night before, and she was wearing the black shoes she'd borrowed from Audra. Instead of buttoning the plain blouse nearly to the collar, she'd left it open so that just a hint of cleavage was visible.

She expected her twin to make some amused comment when Ali walked past Audra's office, so she wasn't surprised when Audra whistled and called out, "Come back and let me get a better look at you."

Ali backed up and struck a silly pose in the doorway. Then she started to walk away again, but Audra rushed after her and snagged her hand before she got very far.

"Don't say anything," Ali warned.

"What? You look nice." Audra pursed her lips, assessing. "The skirt length is a big improvement and, of course, I like the shoes since they are mine. Will I be getting them back anytime soon, I wonder?"

"I'll pay you for them. How much?"

Audra rattled off a figure that left Ali's head feeling light. "For shoes? God, you're insane."

"I take my footwear seriously, but no need to pay me. You can consider them a gift." Audra stepped closer then and fussed with Audra's blouse, undoing yet another button before unfastening the decorative belt around her own waist and wrapping it around Ali's.

She stepped back afterward and nodded in approval. "It works for now, but I still want to take you shopping for a wardrobe overhaul. I'd prefer Milan or even Rodeo Drive, but I'll settle for a midweek daytrip to Chicago. What do you say?"

"Maybe."

Audra grinned. "I'll take that as a yes since the last six times I've suggested such a thing you refused outright."

"Whatever," Ali said, but then she gave her twin's hand a squeeze. "Thanks for the belt."

"You're welcome. Good luck."

Her sister's salutation struck Ali as odd until she opened the door to her office. She had figured she would run into Luke at some point since she knew he hadn't checked out of the resort yet. But she hadn't expected to find him seated at her desk with his size eleven feet propped on the tidy blotter.

He smiled. "Good morning."

She frowned. "It's Monday and you're sitting in my chair. What's good about it?"

Undeterred by her surly tone, he held out a mug of coffee. "Audra said you were cranky before you had your first cup."

Ali closed the door behind her, set her purse on the credenza and then leaned against it. "What do you want now? Any more conspiracy theories to share with me?"

"I figure I owe you an apology for that…and the other things I said about your, uh, boyfriend. I'm sorry."

That took the wind out of her sails, even though he had said as much after she'd stormed out of the restaurant. She told herself it was only because he was offering coffee and she hadn't had time for a cup yet that morning.

She nodded stiffly. "Apology accepted. Now, if you don't mind, I have work to do."

"Me, too. I'm flying back to New York. I have a meeting with a business associate about a deal we have in the works. I'll be back this evening, though. Maybe I'll see you later."

She left him with the same qualified response she'd given Audra. "Maybe."

And, like Audra, Luke looked just as pleased.

Ali got in late that evening. Exhausted, she changed into a comfortable button-down blouse and a pair of jeans and rooted around in her cupboards for something easy to make for dinner. It was looking like tuna fish on whole wheat, but a nicely grilled T-bone sounded better.

When she'd walked out to get the mail earlier, she'd smelled the mouthwatering scent of sizzling beef and charcoal wafting on the chilly evening breeze. Luke, she decided. He was back. She supposed he was down at his grandmother's right now, perhaps sorting through Elsie's things. His business, she told herself, even though she had offered to help.

She was cutting a few fat slices of bread when he knocked at her kitchen door.

"I decided to take you up on your 'maybe' and ask you if you'd like to have dinner."

She crossed her arms and leaned against the door-jamb. "One meal with you was enough, thank you. I still have indigestion."

"I thought you had forgiven me for that."

"I forgave you. It doesn't mean I plan to subject myself to it again."

"Not even for steak?"

She glanced back at the can of tuna and moistened her lips. What could it hurt? If he did something to really tick her off, she would be within walking distance of home this time.

"I'm listening."

"I picked up a couple of Delmonicos. I just removed them from the little charcoal grill I bought at the store in town."

"How'd you get all that out here on your Harley?"

He shrugged. "I rented a car when I got back to the island this afternoon." Glancing over his shoulder at the dark clouds, he added, "It looked like rain."

Ali didn't want to discuss the weather. "Let's get back to those steaks. How did you cook them?"

"Medium rare."

Her stomach rumbled again, but she would be damned if she would make this easy for him.

"What do you have to go with them?"

He scratched his chin. "Well, that's the thing. The deli was out of potato salad so I picked up one of those pasta-in-a-box side dishes at the grocery store. You know, the kind that you can make in less than ten minutes on the stovetop."

"But you don't have any electricity."

"Exactly."

She heaved an exaggerated sigh. "I've got potatoes. I can throw a couple in the microwave to bake and be over in ten minutes."

He grinned. "Do you have sour cream and chives?"

"Don't push your luck."

Even so, as Luke backed away from her door he asked, "You wouldn't happen to have the makings for a nice Caesar salad?"

Her gaze narrowed. "God, Banning. Do you at least have plates, silverware and napkins?"

His brow crinkled. "Nothing that's not coated in dust and no water to wash them with."

"Are you inviting me to dinner or are you trying to scam a free meal off me?"

He offered a sexy half grin and pointed out, "I spared no expense on the meat, and I've got a really nice bottle of Beaujolais to go with it."

"But no clean wineglasses, I suppose."

His head tipped to one side. "Ah, no. No wineglasses and, now that I think of it, no corkscrew, either. Elsie wasn't much of a drinker."

"Why don't you bring the steak and wine here, since I'm providing everything else? But I'm not doing the dishes."

"Does that mean you're no longer angry about the other day?" Luke asked.

Ali shook her head. "No. It means I'm hungry and steak sounds good, especially since somebody else cooked it and paid for it and will be cleaning up the mess afterward."

They ate at her kitchen table with the overhead light chasing away the gloominess of the encroaching night. Outside the wind had picked up, throwing dirt and debris at her newly cleaned windows, and fat clouds made it darker than normal for that time of evening.

"A storm's coming," she murmured, slicing off a sliver

of meat. He hadn't been kidding about the quality of the steak. It melted in her mouth.

Luke gazed out the window. "I've never liked storms."

Ali knew that. And she knew why. His father had been found dead on the side of the road after one. It hadn't been nature's fault alone that Roger Banning died. More appropriately the blame belonged to the seven shots of whiskey he'd consumed before leaving a tavern near the ferry dock.

His car had struck a tree and the elder Banning had crawled out, attempting to walk home during the wicked electrical storm that had already cut phone lines and power to most of the island. They found his body the next day. He'd drowned in six inches of water after passing out in a ditch. Luke was nine at the time, a young and frightened boy. And he'd spent the stormy night alone in the dark, waiting for his father and worrying that he might have left the same way Luke's mother had, going out one day and just not coming back.

Ali wanted to reach over and squeeze his hand in comfort now. But that wasn't what he really needed. He would think it was pity, and he detested pity. So she kept the conversation going instead.

"I loved storms when I was a girl. I'd lie in bed, listening to the waves breaking on the shore and the wind rustling the leaves, and I'd count the seconds between the flash of lightning and the crash of thunder."

Luke seemed to shake off his melancholy. "You always were a weird kid," he snorted.

"Just for that I'm not going to help you with the dishes."

"That's okay. I'm going to leave them for the maid," he teased.

But Ali was serious when she asked, "Do you have one of those back in New York?"

He nodded.

"And a cook, too, I suppose."

"Yep, and a driver."

"For your motorcycle?"

"No." He chuckled. "For my car. I don't get to ride the Harley very often. Too much traffic and too many stoplights in Midtown to make it any fun."

She'd read dozens of magazine articles about his free-wheeling Manhattan lifestyle, a fact she would share with him only under threat of torture. She'd seen him, too, in the accompanying photographs, dressed in tailored suits and crisp shirts, and looking far different from the rough and tumble boy he'd once been.

"Do you like New York?"

"I love it. I can't imagine living anywhere else. Sometimes it's as if the place itself is alive. There's so much energy and excitement all the time."

"It sounds exhausting."

"Well, it's not like Trillium. It's so laid-back here." But then he frowned, and she wondered if he'd finally realized that was part of the island's charm.

"Audra used to say the same thing about living in

L.A. Neither one of you could appreciate what people pay good money and travel for miles to find here."

"What is that exactly?"

He sounded sincere in his curiosity and so she answered him. "Peace and tranquility. As a side benefit, they can enjoy nature's beauty and appreciate the way it's always changing and renewing itself."

He didn't say anything for a moment, then, "Well, Audra seems awfully happy these days. Island life must agree with her now."

"I think she had her fill of Hollywood excitement. I know anyone who picked up a tabloid got their fill of it," Ali said wryly, thinking back to the days when her sister had set tongues wagging across the globe with her ribald antics. "And, of course, there's Seth. He's not from here originally, but he doesn't want to leave. He absolutely loves it here. They just finished building a big house on the northeastern tip of the island. They said they want to be able to watch the sunrise from their bedroom window every morning."

"Love gives you roots, I guess."

"I thought it was supposed to give you wings," Ali replied. She rubbed one of her index fingers slowly around the rim of her nearly empty wineglass, thoughtful for a moment. "So, do you have 'roots' back in New York?"

One side of his mouth quirked up. "Are you asking if I'm seeing someone, Alice?"

"Never mind," she snapped.

"No, no." He was smiling fully now. "I'm more than happy to satisfy your curiosity."

"I just figured you poked around in my private life, why shouldn't I do a little poking around in yours?"

"That's fair enough, I suppose." He reached for the wine bottle and refilled both of their glasses. Afterward, he said, "I'm not in a serious relationship with anyone."

She picked up her wine, sipped. "Define 'not serious'."

He didn't hesitate, as if he had set up quite rigid boundaries when it came to members of the opposite sex. "No commitment and no expectations of one in the foreseeable future."

The words made her sad. And yet Ali felt as if she were looking in a mirror. Had not her personal life turned out the same? With one major exception, she supposed, adding, "I'm assuming that doesn't keep you from sleeping together."

Luke sipped his wine and said nothing.

"It sounds cold."

He shrugged. "I prefer to think of it as casual. It suits me."

But after he said it, Luke wondered if it really did, just as a moment earlier he'd wondered when Manhattan's megawatt charm had started to dim for him.

As good as his word, he cleared the table when they were through with their meal, and although he hadn't so much as rinsed out a cereal bowl in too many years to count, he found himself standing at Ali's sink, feeding the remnants of their meal to the garbage disposal and arranging the dirty plates in the dishwasher.

The work brought back memories of standing in his grandmother's kitchen, helping out after dinner, and he nearly smiled. No fancy dishwasher for Elsie. She would wash and Luke would dry as she told him amusing stories about his dad's boyhood, stories intended to make Luke remember the man Roger Banning had been before alcohol had taken over and ruined his life. All of her efforts, however, couldn't change the fact that when a lot of the folks on the island regarded Luke all they saw was the town drunk's son.

"I think that plate is rinsed enough," Ali said, intruding on his thoughts.

"Hmm?" Luke turned.

She nodded toward the plate he held under a stream of warm water. "I think that plate is plenty rinsed."

He glanced down. "Oh." After shutting off the water, he stowed it in the dishwasher.

"Detergent is under the sink. Whatever you do, don't use the regular dish soap or we'll be wading through bubbles like something out of a sitcom."

"You sound as if you're speaking from experience."

"Dane," she said simply.

Luke laughed outright.

When he'd completed the task and switched on the machine, he turned. Ali was still seated at the table, finishing her wine with her stocking feet propped up on the chair he'd vacated. She didn't move her feet when he came back to the table and so after drying his hands on a dish towel, he scooped them up, sat down and plopped them back in his lap.

She tried to pull them away, but he held firm and when he began to massage the instep of the right one, she groaned low and gave up all effort to resist. That's when he swallowed hard and found himself lost in memories again, these ones much more erotic than the last batch that had featured his grandmother.

He ran his hand up her calf and worked down one sock, revealing smooth skin and a trim ankle. Then he tugged it off completely. God, she had sexy feet, narrow and fine-boned. Her toenails were still painted the vivid red that had driven him to distraction during their meeting in Saybrook's conference room. Had that really been just last week? A lifetime seemed to have passed since his return.

He glanced up and she was watching him, tawny eyes wary and her breathing just this side of labored. He stroked one arch with his thumb and for the briefest moment her eyelids fluttered shut before her gaze widened again as he pushed the cuff of her pants up to her knee, revealing more smooth skin.

Just as the steak had been too good to resist, he raised the limb to his mouth and dropped a kiss onto her shin, moving lower afterward until he reached the brown beauty mark just above her ankle.

Ali felt the pressure building inside her, heat seeming to simmer out of her every pore. She should pull away and put an end to this…this… My God! It was foreplay. But she didn't. She couldn't. She reached for her wine, hoping to act nonchalant even as her pulse was revving like an Indy car on the final lap of the big race. Then Luke's tongue flicked across the birthmark on her ankle and she arched back on a moan, spilling wine down the front of the oversize chambray shirt she wore and nearly kicking him square on the chin.

He stopped. He smiled. And she supposed it was just as well that the electricity sputtered off at that point, because she knew her face was heating to the same color as the Beaujolais. She hurriedly set her feet back on the floor and rose.

"I'd better go soak this shirt or the stain will set." The words were practical, and yet her voice was a nearly unrecognizable whisper.

"Ali—"

"I th-think I have a flashlight in the cupboard over the stove, if you want to get it while I'm changing."

But when she tried to walk past Luke, he snagged her hand and forced her to stop. She could just make out his features in the nearly dark kitchen. His eyebrows were raised in question as he pressed her palm to his lips and kissed it. His breath was warm. She remembered that heat. God help her, but she yearned to feel it again. She reached out and stroked his cheek, which was rough with a day's worth of stubble, and then she couldn't stop herself. She bent and kissed him full on the mouth.

One kiss. That was all she intended while her need was safely obscured in the room's shadows. Afterward, she would end their evening and send Luke on his way before she did something she truly regretted. That was the smart thing to do, the practical thing, after giving in to this bit of insanity. But his apparent hunger fed hers. Even as their kiss deepened, she felt his fingers tugging at her shirt, working free the button closest to her throat before moving on down to the next one. His hands made quick and efficient work of the task even as his tongue took its time exploring her mouth.

"Ali," he murmured afterward, trailing his lips down her neck and she was lost.

Gone was the commonsensical woman who'd made it her mantra to look before leaping. Passion beckoned, obliterating all else. Ali shocked them both by straightening, but only so she could hoist a leg over his lap and straddle him as he sat on the chair.

Forget practicality. Forget sanity. She knew what she wanted. It had been so long. More than a decade of need boiled over inside—consuming her, consuming them both as Luke parted her shirt. He hesitated then and Ali framed his face between her trembling hands, kissing him again. Cloaked in darkness, she was bold, nipping at his lower lip and sighing out his name. When the kiss ended, she arched back again until the edge of the table bit into her spine. Luke needed no more invitation. He was pushing the lace of her bra aside when the overhead light flickered back on, illuminating the kitchen in harsh reality.

Ali didn't need to see herself reflected in his eyes to know the picture of reckless abandon she made with her shirt gaping open and her hair tumbling about her shoulders.

What was she thinking? That if sex happened during a power outage it didn't count? And here she had berated Luke for his casual relationships just minutes before and yet what more could come of this than heartache?

She tried to scoot off his lap and, in truth, she might have even run from the room, appalled as she was by her behavior. But Luke didn't allow her the option. He did something that for all of its chivalry and good sense still managed to break her heart. He rebuttoned her shirt, helped her to her feet and then he left.

CHAPTER SEVEN

THEY somehow managed to avoid one another throughout the rest of the week and Ali was never so happy to have the weekend arrive. She had another date with Bradley that Saturday evening and she had considered canceling it. After what had gone on in her kitchen with Luke, she felt she should. She still blushed every time she recalled the way she had tossed a leg over his lap and arched back against the table.

But in the end she didn't cancel the date. Memories of Luke had caused her to cancel too many dates. She could see that now. She could see the way she'd been in a virtual holding pattern for the better part of eleven years, waiting for him to return to the island and tell her that he'd made the biggest mistake of his life by walking away.

Well he was back, although not for good. And while he'd made it clear he still wanted her, it was plain he didn't regret leaving.

I can't imagine living anywhere else, he'd said of New York.

The truth was leaving hadn't been a mistake for him. He'd made a different choice, chosen a different road, just as it had been Ali's choice to stay on Trillium when she could have gone after him or gone anywhere else for that matter. She hadn't, because to her the island was more than an isolated hunk of rock and soil cropping out of the vast lake that girded Michigan's western boundary. It was her home, her center, the one place where she felt complete and at peace.

Ali and Luke might be on speaking terms once again but that didn't change the fact that for him Trillium was not a paradise but a prison of unhappy childhood memories from which he was glad to be free. She would be wise to remember that.

And so she prepared for her date.

Audra showed up at the cottage just after Ali stepped out of the shower. She strolled into the bathroom and plopped down on the edge of the big claw-foot tub while Ali toweled the excess water from her hair.

"Hot date tonight?"

"Bradley will be here in about thirty minutes. We're having dinner at the resort."

They were dining at Saybrook's at his suggestion. He'd never eaten at the resort and wanted a chance to sample the offerings of their new chef, whom the Conlans had courted away from a mainland restaurant.

Audra frowned. "You're having dinner with Bradley? You're seeing him tonight?"

"Who else would I have a hot date with?" Ali challenged.

"I just thought… Luke's been spending his evenings out this way. I assumed…"

"He's working with Tom Whitey on repairs and I think he's had a surveyor out. He's selling the property and maybe splitting it into a few parcels."

"But—" Audra began.

Ali cut her off. "There's nothing going on between us. Nothing," she repeated, even as the scene from the kitchen replayed itself in intimate detail. In the mirror, Ali watched her face flush scarlet. Beyond her reflection, Audra's eyebrows inched up.

"I wasn't aware 'nothing' could make you blush," she pointed out.

Ali tugged a comb through her hair, ruthlessly yanking at the knots rather than trying to gently untangle them. "There will always be…attraction between us," she agreed. "But that's all and it's not enough." Her vision misted. "Damned knots," she muttered.

Audra rose and took the comb from Ali's hands and then pushed her onto the closed toilet seat. Audra's strokes were even and sure as she worked the comb through Ali's hair from the part all the way to the ends.

"You've loved him since we were girls," Audra said after a moment.

"And now I need to move on," she admitted quietly. "He did. A long time ago."

"Are you so sure?"

She nodded. "Aud, you've been right. I wasn't over him. I don't think I realized how trapped I've been in the past until he came back. But now I've seen him again and I've had…I guess you'd call it closure."

Audra groaned. "I ought to take the pair of you and knock your heads together. That's what I ought to do. God, I can't believe you two. Ask yourself this, Alice, if he's so over you, why hasn't he married? The guy has had ample opportunities."

"He's not interested in commitment."

"And why do you suppose *that* is?"

Ali shrugged. "I guess because his mother abandoned the family when he was a child."

Audra let out a strangled cry. Waving the comb under Ali's nose, she said, "Stop with the psychobabble already. That's crap and you know it. Luke hasn't married because he still loves you."

Ali rose.

"Where are you going?"

"To get dressed. Bradley will be here soon."

Audra sighed dramatically in defeat. "So, what are you going to wear?"

Forty minutes later, Audra had gone and Ali waited for Bradley on the front porch of the cottage. He was late, which was just as well. She was hardly waiting in eager anticipation for his arrival, although she had to admit, she looked good thanks to Audra.

She'd left her hair loose. Audra had showed her how to use the blow dryer and a fat rounded metal brush to make its usually unruly ends behave. And her sister had applied Ali's makeup, insisting on a little more eyeliner than Ali would have used on her own. She liked the resulting look, the way it made her eyelids look longer, heavier. Of course, she would never admit as much to Audra.

She would have pulled on a sweater set and a pair of her trademark khakis, but Audra had refused to let her leave the cottage "dressed like some prep school dropout." In the end, giving in had seemed like much less trouble.

Ali had to admit, her sister certainly knew how to scrape together an outfit, pairing Ali's classics in such a way that she looked almost trendy. It helped that Audra had added a few of her own touches. She'd dumped out the contents of her slim black handbag and then had given Ali the shoes off her feet. And so Ali found herself wearing one of her plain blouses, unbuttoned far enough to reveal a tantalizing peak of the lacy black camisole Audra had found stashed in the back of one of Ali's bureau drawers. The black pencil skirt, even hemmed, would have been too conservative on its own, but Audra's leopard print pumps added a touch of the wild just as their dagger heels added a good three inches to Ali's height.

When Bradley was officially forty minutes late, she gave up pacing the length of the porch and decided to water the impatiens she'd planted in a pot the day before. She had a feeling she looked like a cross between Martha Stewart and Madonna when the Mercedes pulled into her driveway. Bradley got out, looking unnaturally tanned for springtime in Michigan. His sandy hair was neatly combed and held in place with what she suspected was some sort of gel. He was dressed impeccably in beige trousers, a white broadcloth shirt and navy sports coat that had a designer insignia stitched on the breast pocket. Put an ascot at his open collar and he'd look right at home at the fancy yacht club over on the mainland.

As Ali stood there holding the watering can she decided that Bradley Townsend probably didn't own a pair of jeans, at least not the kind made of durable denim, and he wouldn't be caught dead on a Harley with the wind making a mockery of his hairstylist's handiwork.

In other words, he was the antithesis of Luke Banning. In fact, every man she'd dated over the past decade had been as different from him as night is from day.

She shook off the thought.

"Sorry I'm late," he said. His gaze wandered down her legs and stopped at the leopard-print shoes. "You look amazing, by the way."

His open appreciation made her uneasy for some

reason and suddenly she regretted letting Audra talk her into changing her appearance.

"Thank you," she murmured. "We'd better go. Our reservation was for six o'clock. I rescheduled for six-forty-five when it appeared you would be late."

Bradley grimaced and apologized again. "I'm never sure about the ferry's schedule."

"No one is," she replied on a smile.

The ferry ran on the hour once the ice melted and on the half hour during peak tourist season. Despite the posted times, it was a well-known fact that the boat left whenever it became full, making the schedule anything but reliable.

"One of the hazards of living on an island, I suppose," Bradley said.

"I prefer to think of it as a charming quirk." Her tone held a challenge, which was ridiculous. But then she'd always felt loyal of the island and protective of it.

His smile came easily. "You're right."

He held open the car door. No motorcycle here to mess with her hair and make conversation all but impossible. This was a classy sedan with leather seats and Vivaldi playing at low volume from the stereo.

Despite their tardiness, she asked Bradley to take the long way to the resort, driving through the state forest and then along the water, where the sun was beginning its descent. They passed Luke's cottage after pulling out of her driveway, and even though she'd told herself not to look, Ali's gaze was pulled there as if by a magnet. His motorcycle was gone and so was Tom's truck. The little house was dark and quiet once more.

"Is that where Luke Banning used to live?" Bradley asked.

Her gaze sliced guiltily away and she cleared her throat. "Yes. With his grandmother."

"Pretty humble origins. I read somewhere that his father died—I think from a drug overdose—and his mother went out for cigarettes and never came back."

"Actually his father died in an accident," Ali said, for some reason deciding to shade the truth. There was no way to shade his mother's abandonment, so she said instead, "His grandmother raised him. She was a lovely woman."

"Did you know him well?" Bradley asked.

"He was friends with my brother," she said, leaving out the more intimate relationship that had developed later.

"Rumor has it he's investing in Saybrook's and that you guys might be considering an expansion."

Bradley's questioning made Ali uneasy as she remembered Luke's contention that the man was interested in the resort.

"I'd rather not talk work, Bradley."

"I'm sorry. I didn't mean to make you uncomfortable. I'm just curious."

After a few minutes, Saybrook's came into view and Ali couldn't stop the sigh that came to her lips. Even though it wasn't full dark yet, the white lights twinkled in the rose garden, and through the French doors that led inside she could see that the dining room was already crowded. Normally, even a Saturday night in May would have been on the slow side, but Trillium High School's prom was that night and so many of the tables were taken up with tuxedo-clad young men and sleekly coiffed young women wearing strapless gowns.

Audra was there, too, her hair pinned up in a messy 'do, her generous curves filling out a designer dress that probably cost more than all of the teens' knockoffs put together.

She breezed up and kissed Ali on the cheek. "Quite a crowd, hmm? Reminds me of when we were kids and used to hide out in the rose garden and peak through the doors hoping to spot stars."

"I didn't realize you were going to be here tonight. You didn't mention it when you were at my house earlier."

"I offered to help hostess until the kiddies head off to the dance at the high school. It was kind of last minute." She smiled coolly at Bradley. "Hello."

"Nice to see you, Audra."

It was a perfectly polite thing to say, and yet something about the quietly issued words set Ali's teeth on edge. Ridiculous.

"Yes. Well, enjoy your dinner."

And after one last smile for Ali, Audra drifted away. Ali couldn't quite explain the odd undercurrent of tension between the two, but it was forgotten as she and Bradley followed the maître d' to their table.

"This takes me back," Bradley said as he held out a chair for her.

"Me, too." A nostalgic smile tugged at the corners of her mouth. When she glanced up, however, the first person she saw was the very man who'd escorted her to her own senior prom thirteen years earlier.

Luke was seated alone at the table behind her and Bradley, apparently having just finished his meal. No yacht club chic for him. He was dressed in unrelieved black. Black slacks, black shirt, complementing his nearly black hair and making the blue of his eyes stand out all the more. His gaze, cool and assessing, was on Ali. Under his scrutiny, her smile became a taut line. She'd known running into him at the resort was a distinct possibility since he was staying there, but she'd hoped, really hoped, to avoid him that evening.

"Everything okay?" Bradley asked, apparently noting her frown.

She dragged her gaze back to her date. "Y-yes, of course. Everything is fine. Shall we start with some wine?"

She picked up a dark leather folder and held it out to Bradley, knowing without looking that Luke was watching her every move.

"The resort carries an impressive selection, I see," Bradley said.

"Yes." She smiled. "Everything from French champagne to California vintages and even some of the cherry wines made in nearby Leelanau."

"What are you in the mood for?" Bradley asked. The smile that accompanied his words was intimate.

Involuntarily her gaze strayed to Luke. One of his dark eyebrows rose, the gesture filled with mocking challenge. Just a few nights ago, she'd straddled his lap with only denim and cotton keeping them apart. As if she needed to be reminded of that. She'd thought of little else since then. And what had he done? He'd buttoned up her shirt for her. The gesture was sweet, but afterward, as she'd lain alone in the dark, her body still vibrating with need, the gesture had seemed less sweet and more like "thanks, but no thanks." Especially since he hadn't so much as dropped by since then even though she'd heard his motorcycle speeding by every evening.

She cleared her throat, decision made.

"I'm in the mood for champagne," she said.

"Oh?" Bradley was surprised, but clearly pleased. He leaned over the table. "Anything in particular you feel like celebrating?"

Ali had never been much good at flirting and she wasn't about to start now, but she did smile and because she could think of nothing else to say, she replied, "I guess we'll see."

It wasn't until she saw the interest flare in her date's eyes and glanced past him to see the muscle tick in Luke's cheek that she realized her words held a promise.

They had just placed their dinner order with the waiter when Bradley's cell phone trilled.

"Sorry. I'll just take this in the lobby," he said, rising to his feet as he unclipped the phone hooked to his belt. "Excuse me."

As soon as he was gone, Luke rose and then slipped into the vacated seat. "Hello, *Alice*."

She gritted her teeth. "Luke. Did you enjoy your dinner?"

"Yes. I recommend the beef tenderloin."

"It is the chef's specialty," she replied, smoothing out the linen napkin spread over her lap to have something to do with her hands.

He leaned back in his chair. "So that's Townsend."

"Yes."

"Hmm."

"What's that supposed to mean?"

"It doesn't mean anything. I just said, 'hmm'."

She fought the urge to roll her eyes. "Come on. I'm sure you have an opinion that you're dying to express. Do it now and save me the suspense."

"You seem well suited."

Ali angled her head. There was an insult in there somewhere, she was sure.

"Well suited?"

"Yes. You even dress alike. Conservative."

"I prefer to think of it as classic."

One side of his mouth lifted. "Okay, classic," he

conceded. "With a new twist tonight. I like the..." His gaze lingered on the V of her blouse and the lingerie peaking out before he said, "Shoes. I didn't think you owned anything quite like that."

"They're Audra's." Without thinking, Ali admitted ruefully, "I'm going to pay later. They're already cramping my toes. It gives a whole new meaning to the phrase 'fashion victim'."

"A good foot rub would remedy that."

She angled up her chin at the reference to the other night, but before she could formulate a suitable reply, he leaned down and snagged one of her ankles and removed the shoe. Then he settled her bare foot between his thighs. She thanked God for the tablecloth, which hid the location of her foot, and the darkened room, which hid the deep stain of her blush.

"What do you think you're doing?" she snarled, determined not to struggle, determined not to moan as his fingers worked the same magic that had made all sense of propriety disappear in her kitchen.

"It's called a foot rub."

"It's called foreplay," she said. And they both knew where it had nearly led the other night. "Let go of me, Luke."

"In a minute." He smiled wickedly. "Then I'll torture us both by doing the other one."

And, damn the man, if that's not exactly what he did, so that afterward Ali's body tingled like one giant exposed nerve and though her feet were once again planted firmly on the floor, she had no idea where her shoes were.

The waiter came by then. He glanced first at Luke and then at Ali. "Should I bring another glass?" he inquired politely.

"No, Jeremy. Mr. Banning won't be joining my party. He just stopped by to say hello while my date is taking a phone call."

The young man nodded and left the champagne in an ice bucket at their table along with two old-fashioned champagne saucers. Then he handed Ali a note from Audra.

"Be sure to drink to closure," it read. "And be sure to get my shoes back."

Ali shredded the paper before tossing the confetti-size pieces into her borrowed handbag. Audra could clean it out, she thought nastily.

At Luke's questioning expression, she waved one hand dismissively. "Just Audra trying to be amusing."

Silence stretched for a moment, and then Luke remarked, "You don't see this style of glass many places anymore." He picked one up and twirled it by the stem. "You know what they say these are modeled after, right?"

Ali shook her head as she glanced toward the French doors. She hated cell phones. What could be so important that her date had spent the better part of fifteen minutes chatting into one? It served him right that when he returned to their table he would find another man not only sitting in his seat, but holding his glass.

"Marie Antoinette's breasts."

Her gaze snapped back at Luke's words. "Excuse me?"

"Champagne saucers." He grinned again. "They're supposedly modeled after Marie Antoinette's breasts."

He hoisted the glass again and watched her over its wide rim. Then his gaze meandered south, making Ali wish she had buttoned the blouse all the way up to her throat. "The perfect size, in my opinion."

She felt her blood pop and fizz with the same effervescence as the freshly poured Dom Perignon. In the low light of the restaurant, with a candle flickering on the table between them and slow music playing low in the background, the years melted away and memories assailed her. She recalled exactly how Luke's work-roughened hands had felt caressing her bare skin. How his smile would slide from sexy to wicked as he'd tempted them both with the urgent promise of more.

"Perfect size," he repeated. "You know, of course, that champagne holds its bubbles better in flutes."

She nearly had to shake her head to clear it of inappropriate thoughts. He was talking about wineglasses and he had her thinking about sex. He'd always been good at that sort of thing.

Her tone was slightly breathy, but she was relieved by the switch in topics. "Yes, but we felt this style suited the resort and the vintage Hollywood feel we've marketed."

"Good call." He glanced around the ornate dining room then. "In fact, I have to compliment you on your restoration efforts. The place looks terrific. Just as I remember it from the summer I worked as a bellhop, only better."

Ali knew that Luke, like Audra, had stayed in some of the finest establishments around the globe, and so she appreciated his words.

"Thank you," she said. "The credit really goes to Audra. She's been invaluable. We put her in charge of the redesign both here and at the cottages. Have you seen them?"

He nodded. "Audra took me around last week. Very nice. I especially like the color combinations she chose for the interiors."

"Audra has a good eye."

He rested his elbows on the edge of the table and leaned forward. "It sounds like the two of you are finally on the same page."

"Most of the time. I'm glad she's back. I missed her," Ali admitted softly.

"I worried that—" He stopped, shook his head. "Never mind."

"No, what did you worry about?"

"I know you guys didn't speak for a number of years after I—" He cleared his throat. "Um, *we*, left. Audra mentioned it when I helped her out with some investment advice after one of her divorces."

He fiddled with the place setting in an uncharacteristic show of nerves before glancing up. "I wondered if I was partly to blame for that."

"You mean because she left with you?"

Luke shifted in his seat. "Not *with* me exactly."

"I know. I think I knew that then, even though I was pretty upset with…her."

Ali kept her tone neutral and her expression bland, even though what she had actually felt at the time was abandoned and betrayed by two of the people she loved the best. Not that she'd ever really thought they'd had an affair, but both had been so eager to leave Trillium, they'd sacrificed their relationship with Ali to do it. Afterward, neither one of them had been around to help her pick up the pieces from the other's desertion.

"Here's to reunions, then," Luke said. He hoisted Bradley's champagne glass to his lips.

"Luke," she admonished. "You can't drink that."

He merely shrugged. "I'll buy the guy another damned bottle."

"But it's Dom Perignon," she sputtered.

Over the wide rim of the glass, Luke gave Ali a look that reminded her that money was no longer a concern for him.

"Drink with me, Ali." His voice was pitched low and his words sounded as much like a dare as they did an invitation.

She didn't reach for her glass. She kept her hands in her lap, fingers knotted together almost painfully.

He sighed and set the glass back on the table. "I'll be leaving tomorrow."

"Tomorrow," she echoed.

Why was it her stomach clenched and her heart felt so heavy upon hearing this news? It was what she'd expected. She was glad he was going. Wasn't she?

Yet she heard herself ask, "What about your grandmother's place. You said you wanted to go through her belongings and clear things out."

"I've handled most of it. The rest can wait a few more weeks."

"So, you'll be back?"

"Yes. There's a lot of unfinished business here," he said, leaving her to wonder if he was talking about the resort, the cottage or their relationship.

He picked up the champagne saucer and said once again, "To reunions."

Lost in his gaze, Ali lifted her glass and surprised them both by drinking to his toast.

CHAPTER EIGHT

LUKE felt restless upon his return to New York. He'd always enjoyed Manhattan. It might also be an island, but it had none of the isolated, laid-back feel of Trillium despite being similar in geographic size. Whether living in a cramped studio near Greenwich Village or a spacious penthouse with a Central Park view, he'd always felt if not at home then at least as settled as he figured someone like him would ever feel. But for the first time in years, he missed that stingy scrap of land jutting from Lake Michigan.

He told himself it was because he'd sorted through some of Elsie's belongings during his trip back, packing up the photo albums and some of his grandmother's other personal effects.

He'd found pictures of himself as a boy, hair too long, grin just this side of defiant, chip firmly in place on his shoulder. In almost all of the pictures that included him, at least one of the Conlans had been present as well: A lanky-limbed Dane or a sassy Audra. And then there was Ali, ducking shyly away from the camera or batting away Luke's hands as he attempted to make rabbit ears over her head.

He'd brought the photo albums back to New York, spending more than a couple of evenings going through them while indulging in a rare midweek cocktail. For the first time in years he let the childhood memories come and he discovered that not all of them were so bad or so bitter.

Especially the memories of Ali.

He stumbled across photos of the two of them that his grandmother had taken after they'd begun dating. God, Ali had been beautiful wearing a simple T-shirt and denim cutoffs while helping him wash his Harley in the driveway.

And sexy as hell in a tomboy sort of way while wiping the dust off her bottom after sliding into third at a high school softball game.

And smart, he recalled, turning the page and finding a shot of her walking across the stage at the high school clad in a navy robe and mortar board and ready to give her valedictory speech to Trillium's graduating class.

He knew now that she had only improved with age.

She haunted his peace. Out of sight did not mean out of mind when it came to Ali Conlan. At least not now.

Where once he'd been able to relegate her, and his feelings for her, to the past, he'd had no such luck since his return to New York. Alone in his penthouse with the sounds of the city muted by several dozen stories of steel and glass, he could still hear the hitch in her breath as she'd slid onto his lap, her skin so heated with passion he was surprised they both hadn't wound up suffering first-degree burns.

After a week of sleepless nights, Luke finally admitted that mere nostalgia had not caused the unprecedented wave of homesickness that had him yearning to return to Trillium.

Getting out of bed, he poured himself a drink and then sat at the desk in his den, flipping open one of the photo albums. Ali smiled up at him.

God help him, but he loved her.

Still.

Always.

It came as quite a shock to realize that, and as an even greater one to figure out that Dane and the rest of the islanders weren't the only ones who'd felt Luke wasn't good enough for Ali. He'd felt that way himself.

In fact, in retrospect, he realized it was a huge part of why he'd left Trillium in the first place, determined to prove his worth. Ali had deserved someone better than the rebellious dreamer he'd been. She had deserved someone as stable and sure-footed and grounded as she was. Someone not tainted by the stench of family scandals. Someone who had not caused Trillium's matrons to shake their heads and sigh in disappointment and disapproval every time they saw her with him.

Luke's thoughts strayed to Bradley Townsend then. He still had nothing on the man, nothing other than what he recognized now as jealousy. If he took that out of the equation, maybe Bradley was just the kind of man Ali needed. Maybe *he* was the man she deserved.

After that adumbration, however, Luke tossed back the last of his scotch. Like hell. He'd made something of himself. He had earned people's respect. Even the islanders who'd once turned their noses up at him were happy now to claim him as one of their own.

Now he just needed to convince Ali to forgive him for the past and take him back.

It was then that he wondered: What if he was too late?

During the weeks after Luke's departure, Ali kept busy at the resort. Michigan's spring and early summer had been warm, and despite predictions about less tourist trade in the state, bookings at the resort were up from the year before. In fact, Saybrook's had posted a No Vacancy sign every weekend since Memorial Day, and occupancy during the week was running just over seventy percent.

Ali sat at her desk and gazed out her office window. Despite the odd discontent she'd felt in recent weeks, she concentrated on the resort and she was pleased with what she saw. Guests were milling around Saybrook's neatly manicured grounds. Some perennials were already in bloom, with the bulk of the color coming from newly planted annuals. The resort looked terrific, freshly painted, scrubbed and restored to the elegant glamour of its heyday. She smiled with pride. Saybrook's was back on the map thanks to some inspired marketing. It was shaping up to be a banner season.

Yet something seemed to be missing.

She refused to believe that something actually might be *someone*. She'd come too far in her life to let that happen again. Instead she chalked up the dull ache around her heart to stress and nerves. After all, Ali was heading up the resort's new golf course. Dane and Audra had agreed that since the idea had been hers, she should be the point person. Besides, Ali was the only one of the three siblings who actually played and enjoyed the game.

Plans for the course's layout were firming up now that the additional acreage had been purchased and the deed officially turned over to the resort.

She'd spent the past two weeks visiting competitors' courses, often playing with Bradley. He was a decent golfer, even if he did cheat, improving his ball's lie and shaving strokes. She supposed it was because without doing those things she would have beaten him. Some men just couldn't stand to lose to a woman, although Luke, she recalled, had never had a problem with the fact she could best him at chess three games out of four. The outings proved safe dates, especially since Ali insisted on meeting Bradley at the courses. It made no sense for him to come over on the ferry and pick her up when they would be heading back to the mainland anyway.

If he sometimes seemed overly interested in the intimate workings of the resort and how the partnership between the Conlans and Luke was set up, she told herself he was just being polite and trying to take an interest in her work. Luke's unfounded suspicions had poisoned her mind, she decided. Besides, if Bradley had only been interested in the property, the point was moot now that the resort owned it.

Still, she couldn't quite discount the doubt she felt that his feelings for her were authentic, even as he hinted he wanted their relationship to deepen and grow. Part of her wanted to break things off. She couldn't see herself making a lifetime commitment to Bradley. But then that was exactly why she decided to continue seeing him. It was time to stop measuring all the men she dated against the man who'd once claimed he would love her forever.

Ali shook off that thought now, determined to focus on work. Sorting through the stack of files on her desk, she pulled out four. She had narrowed the list of golf course designers substantially, in part based on their suggestions for how best to put a golf course on an island situated in one of the largest bodies of fresh water on the planet.

She had a conference call set up with a course designer from California who had been one of the PGA's hottest players when he'd been on tour. These days he occasionally showed up on the seniors' circuit, but mostly he concentrated his efforts on building new courses both in the States and abroad. He favored very natural, low-maintenance designs, using existing elements and native flora to enhance play and challenge players. Her fingers were crossed that their initial discussion would go well.

First, however, she would be phoning Luke to bring him up to speed on the latest developments.

Most of the communication she'd had with him since his return to New York had been via the Internet. Thank God for e-mail, she thought. She'd kept the messages she'd sent him short, impersonal and professional. She was still burning with embarrassment—not to mention an appalling amount of need—whenever she thought of their kitchen interlude or the way he'd raised his glass to reunions when he stopped at her table in the resort's dining room that last night. She hadn't been able to eat a meal in either place since then without growing warm and uncomfortable.

Luke kept his missives short and impersonal as well, although the way he signed the last several had left her curious. No Luke, no initials. He simply ended them with *Yours*. Still, he never strayed from business topics. With the exception of the last e-mail in which he'd made a rather interestingly phrased reference to the merits of soft-spike shoes that had left Ali fanning her face afterward and thinking about anything but golf cleats.

She checked the time, took a deep breath and then dialed his business number.

"Ali Conlan to speak with Mr. Banning, please," she said when a receptionist answered.

"Yes, he's expecting your call. Just one moment," the woman said, putting Ali on hold. She didn't miss the irony that as she waited for Luke to pick up, Faith Hill's voice sang through the receiver, pleading with the man she loved to let her let go.

Finally Luke came on the line.

"Hello, Ali."

"Hi."

"Missing me?"

There was a smile in his voice. She pictured him wearing that sexy grin that never failed to send heat shimmying up her spine. But she chose to ignore it, just as she chose to ignore his question.

"I'm calling with a status report, per your request."

"Is that a yes or a no?" he teased.

Again, she ignored him, launching into a monologue on course designers and an artist's rendering of the new clubhouse that would be built where the back nine of the golf course ended.

Afterward, he said, "It sounds like you've kept yourself busy."

"If we want to have everything in place to break ground next spring and have the course up and running by the next season, I can't afford to drag my feet."

"How are they, by the way?"

"How are what?"

"Your feet."

"They're fine," she replied crisply, even as her pulse revved.

"Glad to hear it. Anyone…massaging them?"

"I don't see how that relates to Saybrook's new golf course."

"Did Bradley wonder about the champagne?"

"Let's leave him out of this," she snapped.

She wasn't about to tell Luke that Bradley had indeed wondered why a second bottle and fresh glass had showed up just as he returned to the table. He'd apologized for the length of his absence, but the evening had seemed strained after that. Ali told herself it had nothing to do with Luke or the way he had insisted on helping her put on her shoes before he'd left Saybrook's dining room. When he passed Bradley on his way out, Luke had paused and turned so that he could send a wink in Ali's direction. Dressed all in black, he'd reminded her of a cat burglar who'd just gotten away with a multi-million dollar heist.

She cleared her throat. "Now, about the course—"

"So, all business, hmm?" he interrupted.

"That is why you finally made it back to Trillium, isn't it? Business."

"I was sure that was the case," he replied, but he sounded anything but convinced now.

"Well, I think that's for the best."

"Do you?" His voice was a seductive whisper that had her thinking about far more than resorts or golf courses.

Instead of answering his question, she decided to turn it around. "Don't you?"

A pause ensued, one so long that Ali wondered if the connection had somehow been lost, but then Luke said quietly, "The only thing I seem to be thinking about these days is that night in your kitchen."

She swallowed hard. "Let's get back to golf."

"Probably a good idea," he conceded.

"I'm inspecting one of our main competitors later today."

"Is inspecting the same as saying you're playing it?" he asked.

She laughed, some of the tension uncoiling from her shoulders.

"What can I say? It's dirty work, but somebody's got to do it. I've played this particular course a few times in the past. It's got some challenging doglegs and interesting pin placements on its greens, but I never paid close attention to most of the design details or how the architect incorporated the use of the lake."

"You sound like you have a real appreciation for the game," Luke said. "I didn't realize you played. In fact, at out first meeting I seem to recall that you said you didn't."

"No, what I said was I didn't have time for games. I still don't," she said curtly.

"My mistake. So, when did you take it up."

"After college." It was petty, but she felt a small jolt of satisfaction when she added, "I was dating a guy who worked as the golf pro at a course just up U.S. 131 from Petoskey."

"Oh? How long did you date?"

"A few months. Then Tony got a job in Myrtle Beach and moved on."

"Did *Tony* give you many pointers?" Luke asked.

Perhaps she was just imagining things, but it seemed his voice had turned tight.

"Enough," she said. And then she couldn't resist replying with a double entendre of her own. "He helped me perfect my stroke, although that didn't take long."

Was that a groan she heard?

"You always were a fast learner as well as a natural athlete."

"I enjoy sports. I've never been afraid to work up a sweat or push my limits. Of course, golf is more about skill than endurance, and it's as mental as it is physical."

She smiled, because this time she was sure she had heard him groan.

"That's been said about other things, too."

"Oh?"

"Like sex."

"But we're talking about golf, Luke," she reminded him, even as heat pooled low in her body.

"Are we, Ali?"

"We are." Her tone was unequivocal, but she had to balance the telephone receiver on her shoulder so that she could twist open the bottle of chilled water that sat on her desk blotter.

"Then come to New York."

"What?" she asked, the bottle poised before her parched lips.

"There's a course here I think you should *inspect*. I'll come with you. Maybe we could even play for…skins."

The interlude in her kitchen snapped front and center in her mind. "Luke, that's not a good idea."

"You told me that one of the designers under consideration is Lou Fozzella. His signature course is fifty minutes outside Manhattan."

"But, I can't—"

"Look, Ali, as the investor of a significant sum of money in Saybrook's, I don't think my request is out of line. You can fly in on Friday, spend a couple days in Manhattan with me. Then you can go home. Strictly business," he promised, although something in his tone left her wary.

She sputtered half a dozen other protests, all of which he overruled. The last thing Luke said before hanging up was: "I'll send my private jet to pick you up."

Luke returned the phone to its cradle and leaned back in his chair, steepling his fingers under his chin.

Ali was coming to New York, where he hoped she

would see him in a whole new light amid the glittering wattage of his adopted city. He wanted her to be proud of him. More importantly, though, by the time she boarded his jet back to Trillium, he was determined to have earned her forgiveness and regained her trust. Perhaps then she would accept what he now knew as irrefutable fact: They were meant to be together.

Ali tried to send Audra in her place, but her twin was adamant in her refusal.

"You're heading up the golf course project. You need to go."

Dane offered to accompany her, but Audra put her foot down on that as well.

"I'm not minding the store while the two of you jet off to the Big Apple," she said. "Besides, Luke asked Ali to come." She winked then. "It's business."

"It better be," Dane muttered.

So late Friday morning Ali drove her car to the island's small airport, which could now accommodate a small jet on its runway thanks to a generous donation from Audra the summer before. Luke's aircraft was already waiting, door opened to reveal the steps that led to the passenger cabin. Ali grabbed her small suitcase from the back seat of her car and wheeled it over.

Luke appeared in the doorway as she approached, and her heart seemed to turn over in her chest. She blamed the unsettling reaction on surprise. She certainly hadn't expected him to be on board. Or to look quite so handsome. He was wearing a suit, although he had loosened his necktie and unfastened the first two buttons on his crisp white shirt.

"Hello," he said as he took her luggage and then helped her up the steps.

"I didn't realize you were coming with the jet." A thought occurred to her then. "You're not flying it, are you?"

"What would you do if I said yes?"

She didn't hesitate before responding. "I'd grab my luggage and get off."

He laughed. "Well, lucky for both of us then that I'm leaving the controls to another pilot today."

"Does that mean you could fly this thing if you wanted to?" she asked.

He nodded. "I'm licensed."

She had to admit, she was impressed.

"You always wanted to learn how to fly," she mused, and she couldn't help but be happy for him that he'd made so many of those seemingly unattainable dreams from his youth come true. Glancing past him, she whistled low. "This sure beats coach."

The cabin boasted six generously proportioned leather chairs, a galley stocked with only the best food and beverages, and a lavatory that made the ones on commercial aircraft a pitiful joke. But it was the rear of the aircraft that really caught her attention. A bed was tucked behind a curtain. The mattress stretched across the rear of the cabin, covered in a satin duvet the same color as the sky. When her gaze connected with Luke's, he raised one dark eyebrow.

"Interested in joining the mile-high club?" he asked.

Even though she was pretty sure he was just trying to get under her skin rather than under the neatly pressed khakis she'd paired with a no-nonsense button-down blouse, she still had to swallow hard before she could ask, "Is that why you have another pilot behind the controls?"

"The FAA frowns on hanky-panky in the cockpit."

Luke grinned wickedly after saying it, and Ali didn't know whether to slap him or laugh with him. In the end, she merely shook her head.

"You're delusional, Banning. Highly delusional."

"I prefer to think of myself as hopeful." He winked. "Make yourself comfortable. I need to have a word with the captain before we get under way."

Not long after he disappeared through the door that led to the cockpit, Ali heard the engines start. The noise crescendoed right along with her frayed nerves. God, she hated flying. Weak-kneed, she settled into the nearest leather seat and strapped herself in, pulling the belt as tight as was possible across her lap without causing internal injuries.

When Luke returned to the cabin, he took one look

at Ali's bloodless fingers gripping the upholstered arm-rests and frowned in concern.

He nodded toward her white knuckles. "I take it you don't like to fly."

"Hate it," she confirmed. "I'd rather be standing hel-metless on the seat of your Harley as it speeds down Palmer Hill."

He whistled through his teeth. "That much, hmm? How about a drink to loosen your nerves?"

"It's not even noon," she protested.

"It is somewhere," he said and crossed to the bar, where he poured her a couple fingers of whiskey.

He chose the seat opposite hers, smiling as he settled into it and handed her the beverage.

"I got that on my last trip to Ireland. I hear it's some of the Emerald Isle's best."

She downed it in a single gulp, gritting her teeth af-terward. Her tawny eyes watered briefly before she low-ered her lids and settled back against the headrest.

"Are you planning to keep your eyes closed for the entire trip?"

"I might open them after takeoff, assuming we don't die in a fiery crash that will make positive identification of our remains impossible."

For someone so practical, her phobia surprised him. "Come on, Ali. Relax," he cajoled, reaching over to pat her hand. It was as cold as ice. "Air travel is safe. In fact, more people—"

"Die in car accidents than aviation disasters," she finished for him. "I know, I know. Just do me a favor and tell me when we're in the air so that I can stop praying."

"How many times have you flown?" he asked several minutes later when they finally leveled off at cruising altitude.

One eye squinted open. "About four times, most recently at Audra's insistence. She has a private jet, too. Or, she did. It was one of the things she got rid of not long after returning to Trillium and simplifying her life."

"I'm sorry, Ali. If I'd known—"

"Tell me about the golf course," she interrupted, rallying valiantly, although she kept her eyes firmly closed. "That should help keep my mind off our impending deaths."

He laughed softly, but then he did as she requested.

"The name is Havenhurst, and it's a 6,900-yard, par 72 located on Long Island. It's hosted a couple of minor tour events. I like the look of it. And I thought we could talk with the greenskeepers. They've had a lot of success with organic fertilizers, pesticides and soil amendments."

"Good. I've been doing a lot of research on that. I'd like the Rebel to be as environmentally friendly as possible. Are we going to play Havenhurst today?"

"No. Tomorrow. I made tee-times for the morning. I thought you might not feel up to golf after the flight, as relatively short as it is. You can do a little shopping this afternoon if you'd like or go to a museum. My car will be at your disposal."

"Where will I be staying? You never did get back to me on the name of the hotel."

For the first time since concocting his plan, nerves assailed him. "Actually, I thought that you could stay… with me."

Her eyes popped wide open then, fear receding behind fury. "You thought *what?*"

"I have four guest bedrooms in my penthouse, Ali. It hardly seemed necessary to book other lodgings when we will be spending so much time together anyway." When she just continued to regard him as if she were considering how best to flay his skin, he added, "Besides, we're both adults."

The mutinous set of her mouth told him she didn't buy his rationale. In truth, he didn't, either, even though he fully intended to respect her privacy and keep his hands to himself throughout her visit.

Unless she explicitly told him differently. And he planned to do his damnedest to ensure that happened. Something told him this was his one shot at convincing her they belonged together.

"I'm not staying in your penthouse, Luke. No way. You can just forget that."

"Don't trust yourself?" he asked.

"God, your ego is as large as ever."

"After that evening in your kitchen it's not the only

thing," he murmured, enjoying the way her cheeks turned pink.

"That was a mistake. One I don't plan to repeat," Ali snarled.

"If you say so."

"I do."

"Then it shouldn't be a problem for the two of us to stay under the same roof—in separate bedrooms, of course."

She opened her mouth to protest, but then snapped it shut. She had backed herself into a corner and she knew it. After that there was no face-saving way for her to refuse his hospitality.

Traveling with Luke Banning definitely had its perks, Ali had to admit. Bypassing luggage pickup at busy LaGuardia International was one of them. As was the fact that he had Ali in a chauffeured limousine heading toward his home in the time it would have taken them to wind their way up to the front of the line of folks waiting to catch a taxi.

She glanced out the tinted windows as the car made its way into the heart of Manhattan on streets choked with honking yellow cabs, cars and diesel-fume-spewing trucks and buses. The sidewalks were filled with bustling pedestrians, all looking eager to finish up the last day of the work week and head home or to the nearest bar for happy hour.

The sheer volume of humanity was staggering, but

no more so than the ways the buildings shot up from the pavement, all but blotting out the sky.

"What do you think?" Luke asked quietly.

"It's something else," she answered, unable to mask the awe she felt.

"The first day I was in New York all I did was walk around looking up." He laughed ruefully. "Of course, that's probably why my pocket wound up getting picked."

She turned away from the window and regarded him across the limo's climate-controlled interior.

"Weren't you…afraid living here all by yourself?"

"Afraid? No." He shook his head. "I'd been alone before, Ali."

She knew that he had been—both as a boy waiting for his father to stagger home and then later as a young man whose only other close relative had died. Why was it, she wondered, that he still seemed so alone now?

"But this city is so huge, so…so impersonal."

"I think that's why I loved it. It accepted me, no questions asked. No one here knew my dad had died a drunk or that my mom had left me and never looked back. No one asked and no one cared. I got a job cleaning offices at night my second week in the city. One of those offices belonged to a big shot businessman who liked to work late. I picked his brain and he let me do some research on his company's computer system. When the time was right, and with some backing from him, I launched my dot-com."

"I still remember the article in *Business Week* about your success." She shook her head. "It was all they talked about over at the Sandpiper until Audra got a recurring bit part on a primetime sitcom. Then it was, *Luke this* and *Audra that*. It was all I heard for weeks on end. My sister and my ex-boyfriend had hit the big time and everybody on Trillium wanted to know what I thought about it."

He grimaced, one side of his mouth lifting in a sardonic smile. "I can only imagine what you told them."

"I probably said something snarky at the time," she admitted. "But I was proud of Audra and you, too. I'm still proud." Ali surprised them both by reaching across the seat to take his hand. "You've come a long way, Luke, and it has nothing to do with bank accounts, private jets or penthouses."

He squeezed her hand and his voice was choked with emotion when he said, "Thank you."

The shackles of the past finally seemed to be falling away, freeing them both.

"You're welcome."

"Ali, will you do me a favor?"

"What?"

"Will you keep an open mind this weekend?"

Her brows pulled together. "An open mind about what?"

Me.

Us.

But he settled on, "The possibilities."

CHAPTER NINE

LUKE'S penthouse home was not at all what Ali expected. Oh, it was grand, both in size and the caliber of its furnishings. She didn't doubt everything from the chrome lighting fixtures that hung from the high ceiling in the kitchen to the odd metal statue that coiled up from the cool black marble floor in the foyer had cost top dollar. But the place, all six thousand square feet of it, seemed so austere, so dispassionate, so absolutely un-Luke.

"Your decor is very…modern," she said as they sat in his living room, enjoying the finger foods and beverages that had just been served by his housekeeper, an efficient but dour-looking older woman whom Ali suspected had last smiled during the Carter administration.

Floor-to-ceiling windows offered a bird's view of the treetops in nearby Central Park, but they also made Ali feel a bit dizzy, as if she were perched up in the clouds rather than sitting on a squat red chair with foot-wide armrests.

Luke studied her for a moment from his seat on the opposite side of a boomerang-shaped coffee table made of glass and chrome. Despite the fact that he had not changed out of his pricey designer suit, he looked as out of place as she felt in her conservative khakis, twin set and penny loafers.

"You don't like it?" he asked, his expression unreadable.

"It's not that I don't like it," she hedged, glancing around again. In her head she heard her mother's admonition about being polite and complimentary to one's host. "It's just not my taste." Or what I remember to be yours, she almost said before finishing with, "It's…it's very, um, modern."

"Yes, I believe we've established that."

His lips twitched and she relaxed a little. Still, she felt compelled to apologize.

"I'm sorry."

"Don't be. It's not exactly my taste, either."

Ali couldn't have said why she felt so relieved to hear that, but she did. It just seemed so incongruous that the man who'd once picked her a fistful of wild wood lilies could now prefer the odd arrangement of metal geometric shapes that served as a centerpiece on his dining room table.

"Did the place come furnished then?"

"No." He glanced around and shrugged. "I gave the interior designer, whom I've worked with on other projects, carte blanche when I bought the place a year ago. I told her to do it up in whatever style she felt best suited the rooms."

"What about your taste?" she asked, amazed that he could spend hundreds of thousands of dollars, if not more, on furnishings, original artwork and accessories, and not want to have more input than signing his name on the sales receipts. On Trillium, he'd had his head together with Tom Whitey for more than a week over basic repairs to his grandmother's cottage.

He shrugged again. "I'm no expert on decorating. Besides, the penthouse is just an investment. I don't spend much time here except to sleep."

She thought of her own home and the way it represented a haven of sorts, a place where she could regroup and recharge after a long day.

"Expert or not, surely you know what you like."

He leaned forward in his low-slung chair and the slow smile that curved his lips sent a shower of sparks ricocheting around in her system, obliterating all thought of home furnishings.

"Oh, I know what I like, Alice."

She cleared her throat, determined to change the subject. "So, what are we going to do?"

"What would you like to do?"

Before she could stop it, her gaze dropped to his mouth and the scene in her kitchen played back. She remembered exactly where she'd wanted those lips. His grin widened. Apparently he knew, too. She glanced away.

"You said our tee-time is in the morning, so that leaves the rest of today."

"And tonight."

She motioned toward his suit. "Do you need to be somewhere?"

"No. I didn't have time to change after a business meeting that ran late this morning. I'm all yours this evening. All yours," he repeated, and she was reminded of the way he had signed his e-mails.

"Luke," she said evenly after managing to swallow. "I'm here in my professional capacity as one of the owners of Saybrook's Resort."

She sounded like a weenie even to her own ears.

"Whatever you say, *Alice.*"

"Luke—"

He held up his hands. "I'm just stating fact here. I canceled my other plans for the weekend once I knew you would be coming to town. I thought this evening we could grab an informal bite to eat at my favorite pizzeria near Hell's Kitchen and then go on a carriage ride through Central Park."

It sounded perfect. And a little too romantic.

"You didn't have to cancel your plans for me. I bought a guidebook and I noticed that we passed several museums and galleries on our way from the airport. I don't want to be any trouble."

His laughter seemed self-mocking. "Ali, you've been nothing but trouble for me since the day you hit puberty."

"Thanks a lot." She was insulted, she told herself, even though she felt oddly flattered.

"I mean that in a good way." Then he sobered. "I thought you had agreed to keep an open mind. Reneging on your promise already?"

"I just don't think we should stray from business."

"Then I have a confession to make. Business isn't the only reason I asked you to come here."

"Luke—"

But he shook his head. "Let me show you my New York, Ali. It's a great city." When she hesitated, he added, "Please. It would mean a lot to me."

Possibilities, he'd said earlier. She swallowed hard. And because he also reminded her so much just then of the troubled young man who'd first stolen her heart, all she could do was nod.

Luke assured her the evening would be casual and she could wear what she had on, but she decided to change. She'd brought a couple of simple outfits, both of which went fine with the practical walking shoes stowed in her luggage. When she opened her suitcase, however, she didn't recognize anything inside it.

There was a note on top.

"Too boring. I made some adjustments. You can thank me later. Love, Audra."

When had she managed this? Ali had stopped by the resort on her way to the airport. Had Audra performed her sleight of hand then? It didn't matter. The deed was done.

Ali wanted to wring her twin's neck, but she found herself murmuring in appreciation instead as she pulled out a little black dress. The cut was simple, timeless. It had capped sleeves and a scoop neck, and a hemline that made the most of Ali's long legs. Audra had paired it with open-toed calfskin pumps and even included some silver jewelry. The entire ensemble was classic yet sexy in a subdued way.

"I owe you one," she whispered, slipping out of her khakis.

Luke was on the telephone when she returned to the living room. His back was to her and so Ali could look her fill. He had changed into a pair of lightweight trousers and a tailored sports coat. He was the picture of urban sophistication standing in front of the huge window. He'd come so far since leaving Trillium and she knew geography was the least of it. During the ride from the airport, she'd finally told him how proud she was of him and the look on his face had left Ali humbled.

He turned then, caught sight of her and his expression this time had a more disturbing effect.

Even though he had been in the middle of a sentence, Luke abruptly ended the call. "I've got to go. I'll deal with it on Monday."

He snapped the cell phone closed and stowed it in the breast pocket of his coat after turning it off.

"I didn't mean to interrupt," she said.

"You didn't."

"It sounded like I did."

He shrugged. "It's a matter of priorities."

His words had her recalling the way Bradley had spent twenty minutes of their date gabbing into his cell.

"Well, then, I'm flattered by your priorities."

"Only a fool keeps a beautiful woman waiting." His intimate gaze caressed the length of her. "You look amazing."

Ali smoothed the dress's skirt and then rested her hands on her hips, trying not to fidget under Luke's frank appraisal. "It's Audra's doing. She messed with my luggage."

"God bless her," he murmured. Then he suggested, "We could eat in."

"Uh-uh. You promised to show me your city," she reminded him.

Luke sighed heavily and she couldn't help but smile.

"So I did."

They ate at a restaurant just outside the actual bound-aries of Hell's Kitchen at a place that boasted red-and-white checkered tablecloths and lighted candles stuck into old Chianti bottles. It was cliché and perfect and the food better than anything Ali could remember ever having.

"How did you find this place?" she asked as she sipped

the last of her wine. It didn't seem the sort of restaurant a multimillionaire came to eat. It reminded her, oddly enough, of the Sandpiper with its relaxed ambiance.

"Claudio, the owner, hired me when I first got here. I bussed tables for him five days a week."

"I thought you cleaned offices?"

"That was my night job. I did this during the day."

"You worked two jobs?"

"Three, actually. I also parked cars for a hotel near Rockefeller Center on the weekends." He grimaced. "I found out pretty quickly that minimum wage doesn't go very far in this city."

"It doesn't go far anywhere," she agreed.

"Which is why you wanted me to finish high school." There was no bitterness in his tone, just acceptance and, surprisingly, maybe a little chagrin.

"I knew the odds of you making a decent living without at least your high school diploma weren't very good." She shook her head and laughed then. "As it turns out, what did I know?"

Luke didn't laugh, though. "No, you were right, Ali. It was a tough way to earn a paycheck. You don't eat well living on arrogance. I got damned tired of macaroni and cheese before I finally got lucky and could afford steak."

Something seemed to shift between them. Old wounds finally healing?

"I wouldn't call it luck," she said. "You were always smart, hardworking and determined."

"I believe you called it pigheaded."

It was her turn to be chagrined. "Whatever I called it, you deserve the success you're enjoying."

"I needed to make something of myself. I had a lot to prove."

"Because of your father," she guessed.

"I thought so at the time." He lowered his voice. "I think I also wanted to prove my worth to you."

That surprised her. "Why?"

"I…I wasn't much of anything back then."

"You were to me," she admitted. Indeed, he'd been her whole world.

They were both quiet for a long moment. Then Luke asked, "Ever wish you could roll back time?"

She nodded. "But there's really no sense in trying to change the past."

"That's my Ali. Always so practical." He laughed softly and reached over to run his knuckles over the slope of her cheek. She trembled at the contact, and that was before he added, "I guess I'll just have to keep working on the future then."

After dinner Luke took Ali on a carriage ride through Central Park as promised. She sat across from him on the faded red vinyl seat, legs crossed demurely at the ankles and hands folded in her lap. She'd done something different with her hair, pulling it back from her face, but not in her usual ponytail since some of it still spilled down her neck. She looked like royalty, like a brunette Grace Kelly touring her new principality. And, to his delight, it appeared she liked what she saw.

Her expression gave away her thoughts. She was by turns impressed, amazed and enthralled—just as Luke had been the first time he'd wandered up Fifth Avenue from the gritty streets of Lower Manhattan and discovered this lush, green oasis amid the skyscrapers and bustle of Midtown.

"I want to show you something, a surprise," he said, and then tapped the driver on the shoulder and whispered his destination.

A few minutes later, the carriage came to a halt next to a large grouping of bronze statues. Ali's brows tugged together in puzzlement as she studied them. Then understanding dawned and she laughed in earnest.

"Oh, my God! It's *Alice in Wonderland.*"

He laughed, too, relieved that she wasn't insulted. As much as she hated to be called by her given name, it was common knowledge on Trillium that she owed it to her mother's fondness for the title character in the children's classic.

"I thought you might enjoy seeing this. The first time I stumbled across it I thought of you."

She smiled at him, and he remembered that day half a dozen years ago so clearly. He'd been out jogging at the time and had taken a different route than usual. After that, he'd altered his route so that he passed it during every run. Sometimes he would stop and find a quiet place to sit so that he could watch little kids scramble up on to the rabbit's head or scale the toadstools to perch in Alice's lap.

"I feel like that Alice right about now," she admitted. "Can we take a closer look?"

"Sure." Luke got out and helped her down. They wandered over and she leaned against a giant bronze toadstool. The Mad Hatter grinned at him over one of her shoulders.

"I wish I had a camera," Luke said. "This would make a great shot."

"I have one. It's in my handbag."

He retrieved her purse from the seat of the carriage and handed it to her. She fished out the camera for him.

"Smile," he said, watching her through the viewfinder.

The one she sent him made Luke want to tug her into his arms and get to work on those possibilities he'd mentioned. And yet once they were back in the carriage, something nagged at him. He couldn't have said why, but even sitting there with her namesake, Ali had seemed out of place. He found himself wondering if a bit of transplanted Michigan trillium would be able to grow in Central Park.

It was dark by the time they returned to his apartment building. After the carriage ride, they had walked for several blocks, talking and sightseeing at her insistence. Ali claimed to need to work off some of that dinner, although as far as he could tell she didn't have an ounce of excess flesh anywhere on her person.

He'd reached for her arm, pulling her back from the curb and possibly saving her from losing her kneecaps to the thick bumper of a speeding taxi whose driver was determined to turn right even though the light had changed to red and pedestrians allegedly had the right of way.

"You need to watch your step around here," Luke had said when she glanced up to him in question.

She'd regarded him for a long, considering moment. "I can see that," she'd said at last.

Afterward, he'd let his fingers skim down the inside of her arm and he'd found her hand, weaving his fingers through hers. He hadn't let go of it since then. Even during the elevator ride to the penthouse he'd held on, stroking his thumb over her knuckles and feeling the heat build and need curl through him as they ascended past floor after floor.

Neither one of them said anything until the doors slid open and they stepped out into his foyer.

"I had a great time tonight, Luke. Thank you."

She let go of his hand then and stepped away, the implication being that the night was now over. How many years had it been since a date for him had ended in a chaste peck at the doorstep—his doorstep, no less? But that appeared to be what was happening here. Maybe that was for the best, he told himself. He needed to figure out how to proceed without spooking her. As it was he was pretty nervous himself.

"You're welcome. I had a good time, too. It's been a while since I played tourist." He tucked his hands into his trouser pockets. "Well, we probably should call it a night. I booked the first tee-time of the day at Havenhurst and it's about an hour's drive to the course."

She smiled, somehow managing to look relieved and disappointed at the same time. Or maybe it was just Luke's ego that needed to believe he saw regret before she'd lowered her gaze.

"Then we'd better say good night."

"I'll walk you to your door," he offered, testing himself, testing both of them, since the door in question led to her bedroom.

Ali had thought he was joking, but a moment later they stood at the threshold to the guest room where she would be sleeping.

"Well," Luke said. "Here we are."

"Here we are," she agreed as butterflies catapulted around her stomach.

He was going to kiss her now, Ali was sure of it. She had seen that look in his eyes before, and more than a time or two it had led to far more than kissing.

Possibilities. The word whispered suggestively through her mind. Even so, she planned to resist the temptation he posed. But when he leaned forward she raised her chin, her hasty resolution already forgotten. His mouth hovered over hers for just a moment before he detoured slightly and dropped a light kiss on her cheek.

"Sleep well," he said afterward.

"You, too."

"Not likely," Ali thought she heard him mutter half under his breath as he turned and walked away. And, damn, if she didn't agree with him.

Since the first time she'd picked up a golf club, Ali had been of the conviction that the game was best played first thing in the morning while the dew was still heavy on the fairways and the only other folks out on the course spoke in low, reverent tones suited to public libraries or churches.

The damp grass didn't do much to enhance her play, but there was a beauty to it all the same that turned golf into a near religious experience in her opinion.

So as they sat in their cart on the asphalt path next to the first tee-box, Ali glanced down the lush sweep of misty grass and smiled. The hole was a straight par 4 with the green visible from the tee-box, easily reachable in regulation if one stayed in the fairway, which was bounded by trees and gorgeous flowering shrubs on one side and a brutal set of sand-filled bunkers on the other.

"It's a pretty course, although if you hook it or slice it, you're going to be in trouble," she commented.

"Yes, but that's what makes it golf. Want to make our round a little more interesting?" Luke asked.

"Skins?" she asked dryly.

He had suggested something similar before, although she'd known at the time that what he had in mind was nothing remotely similar to the game in which golfers competed for cash on individual holes.

"In a way." He reached out and fingered the collar of her shirt and his voice dipped to a near whisper when he asked baldly, "Ever play strip golf? One piece of clothing off every time you wind up in the rough."

His devilish grin had her tingling from nose to toes, but she managed to laugh anyway, because his suggestion was so outrageous. Completely outrageous. The stuff of…fantasies.

"You're just hoping to break my concentration," she accused hoarsely.

"That's not all I'm hoping, Ali."

She glanced back to the fairway and decided to play obtuse. "I have no problem sweetening the pot. How about best net total wins and the loser buys a round of drinks in the clubhouse?"

"You call that sweetening the pot?"

"What did you have in mind, besides having the pair of us shed our clothing on our way to each green? That, by the way, would likely get us arrested."

"Among other things," he murmured seductively. Then, "I don't know. Let's make it winner's choice. If you were to win, what would you like?"

She shrugged, but a thought came to her and before

she could censor it, she blurted out, "A foot massage. I'd want you to, um, rub my feet."

"Rub...your feet." A pair of dark brows winged up. "Hmm, what was it that you called it the last time I was massaging your instep?"

Foreplay.

But she said nothing now and he ran a finger along the underside of her jaw. Tipping her chin up, he said, "From where I'm sitting it looks like we both could win if you manage to best me."

"And if you win?" she asked quietly. "What would you want then?"

The look he gave Ali had her moistening her lips, but his words made her mouth go dry.

"I'd want you." He held out a hand then. "Deal?"

I'd want you. What exactly did Luke mean? And because the possible interpretations left her as terrified as she was touched, she decided she wanted clarification. "I'm not s-sure I understand."

"I think you do."

He reached for her hand, but instead of shaking it, he raised it to his lips and kissed the sensitive center of her palm.

He murmured something against her skin. Had it been her name? Or had it been "Always"?

The details of their bargain wound up being moot. As nice as the day had started, it clouded over by nine o'clock and they wound up being rained out before the last four holes of the eighteen could be played. For the remainder of the day, however, Ali's thoughts kept straying to their bet and the intense way in which Luke had regarded her when he'd whispered: *I'd want you.*

They got in late that evening. Luke had taken her out on the town once again, although their destinations were a bit more upscale than they had been the previous night. Thanks to Audra's meddling efforts, Ali again had something appropriate to wear to dinner at the five-star French restaurant Luke had selected. Afterward, they took in a Broadway show and Luke's clout managed to get them not only the best seats in the theater but entry to a closed cast party after the curtain fell.

Once more, Luke was the perfect gentleman, walking her to the door of her bedroom, but before he turned to leave this time, he tugged her into his arms and gave her a kiss so heated and urgent she was surprised it hadn't set off the penthouse's sprinkler system.

"I want to be with you tonight, Ali," he sighed into her hair as he held her afterward, his fingers drawing lazy circles on the small of her back. She was catapulted back in time to the first time they'd made love.

She'd been eighteen and offering up her virginity as they'd clung together on a blanket on a deserted stretch of beach. Overhead, the stars had winked and the moon had bathed them both in silver. Luke had stilled her inexperienced hands as they'd fumbled with the buttons on his jeans, even though he'd been desperate to be with her.

"Are you sure? I don't want you to regret this," he'd said.

She hadn't. Then. But she would now. She was no longer a virgin, but she had plenty to lose where Luke was concerned. And so even as her body burned and begged for release, she said, "I don't think that would be a good idea. I'm…I'm leaving in the morning."

"Stay with me."

They were three words that made Ali ache, for hadn't she once asked him the very same thing?

"I can't." She stepped away from him. "I need to get home."

"Home." He nodded, and something in his expression made her think of the lost young man he'd once been. She reached out a hand to him, but he had already turned and was walking away.

Alone in her room, Ali sank onto the edge of the platform bed, stared at her reflection in the black-framed mirror and called herself a dozen kinds of fool. She'd let the one thing happen that she'd sworn she wouldn't allow: She'd fallen in love with Luke Banning all over again.

CHAPTER TEN

LUKE was quiet as the limousine took them to the airport the following morning. Ali was going home.

Home.

While taking her around New York Luke had discovered a rather painful truth. After years of building a reputation and a career as a savvy businessman, he had precious little to show for his long hours and hard work. Oh, he had lots of *things*—a pricey collection of modern art, land holdings sprinkled around the globe and enough money to live comfortably even if he never worked another day in his life. But he didn't have anyone with whom he could share it. He still didn't have what felt like a permanent place where he could settle in and find peace.

Be happy, his grandmother had beseeched him as she lay dying. *Make me proud.*

Elsie wouldn't be proud, for this wasn't what she'd meant. She'd known his happiness would never be found in business ventures or material possessions. He'd spent millions of dollars on a showplace of a penthouse in Manhattan, but he didn't have a home. And he never would without Ali.

He needed to rectify that. Now. He turned to the woman he loved, the woman sitting beside him, intent on baring his soul. But before he could speak, she said, "I can see why you love it here. New York suits you."

But it didn't suit her. Still, he wanted to know, "Did... did you enjoy yourself?"

"I loved visiting you. Maybe...maybe Audra and I will come back for a weekend some time. She's been trying to get me to go shopping."

Visiting. That's not what he had in mind. He reached for her hand. "I don't want you to be a visitor in my life, Ali. I want so much more than that. Do you understand what I'm saying?"

Yes, she thought she did. And tears threatened. New York was Luke's home now. Hadn't he made that clear with the quiet pride in which he'd shown it off to her? *Stay with me,* he'd urged her last night. God help her, but as much as she loved him, she couldn't.

She'd spent the past decade working toward her dream of running Saybrook's. She was part-owner now and heading up its expansion. Her life was there. His was here. The past, it seemed, was repeating itself.

Ali pulled her hand free and fiddled with the clasp on her watch before she finally felt composed enough to say, "I'm sorry, but I don't think this will work."

"Why not?"

"I can't stay in New York. I'd feel so…" She gestured with her hand as she groped for the right words. "So lost, so swallowed up. I'd miss sunsets on Lake Michigan and the way the air smells like the inside of a cedar chest on hot summer evenings. I'd even miss swatting at mosquitoes if it meant I'd also have to give up listening to the mourning doves cooing to one another before the sun makes it up over the trees. I'm an islander, Luke. You're…so much more than that now."

"I can see I've screwed this up royally." His accompanying laughter was harsh. "I'm not asking you to stay in New York. I don't expect you to move here. What if I told you I'm thinking about relocating?" He cleared his throat. "To Trillium."

The air seemed to back up in her lungs, and so it was a moment before she was able to ask, "What are you saying exactly?"

"I want you back, Ali. I love you."

She almost threw her arms around him before her practical side reasserted itself. He'd been in love with her when he left Trillium the first time, too. Love hadn't stopped him from pulling up stakes then. Love hadn't brought him back to Trillium more than a decade later, either. A business deal had. What if he found the need to move on again? She didn't think she could bear it a second time.

Self-preservation had Ali tugging her hand from his.

She'd never realized she was a coward, but she just couldn't leave herself open to the kind of heartache he'd once caused.

"Trillium can't compete with New York, Luke."

"It's not a competition, but even if it were, I love you. That pretty much trumps everything else. Tell me you don't love me, Ali."

"Luke, please." It came out a near sob, because they'd had this same argument once before, only in reverse. "Don't do this. It nearly killed me when you left Trillium. I didn't think I'd ever get over you. In fact, I don't know that I ever have." The admission was hard, stripping away the last of her pride. "I hope you'll understand, but I don't think I can risk that kind of pain again."

"It's not a risk," he promised.

"It seems like one to me."

She hadn't realized she'd begun to cry until he reached out to wipe a tear from her cheek.

"God, Ali, I'm sorry. I'm so sorry that I hurt you." Swearing under his breath, he fished the handkerchief from his breast pocket and held it out to her. "I want to make you happy. I want to make us both happy. I want—"

But she laid a finger over her lips before he could finish.

"Let's not argue anymore, okay? That got us no-where eleven years ago. It didn't change anyone's mind." She sighed with regret. "It just left us both bitter and angry. I don't want to be either any longer. We're different people, with different needs. I think it's time we both accepted that, made peace with the past and moved on."

But Luke was shaking his head even before she finished speaking. "You're what I need. As for the past, I don't give a damn about it. What do I have to do to convince you that it's the future I want to talk about? You're going home, Ali. I want to, too."

They had arrived at the airport, and the driver opened the door. Ali got out, but when Luke tried to follow, she stopped him.

"Trillium's no longer your home, Luke. Don't come with me."

"I'm coming," he said tightly. "At the very least, let me see you back. I know how much you hate to fly."

"No. Please, stay here." The way her voice broke and her eyes pooled stopped him. She looked so broken…it nearly killed him to know he'd done that to her.

She finally managed to clear her throat. "I need to be alone right now. In fact, I'd appreciate it if you wouldn't come to Trillium for a while. I know you have business there now, but—"

"I don't give a damn about business!" he shouted. "None of that is as important to me as you are."

Her smile was at odds with the tears on her cheeks when she said, "Goodbye, Luke."

"It's not goodbye," he insisted, but she was already walking away.

* * *

Luke didn't overindulge when it came to alcohol. He didn't believe in it given how his father had died. But he poured himself a third glass of scotch that evening and stared out at the glittering skyline that had once held so much promise and appeal. Now it mocked him.

He now knew with painful certainty that nothing would ever fill him with the sense of rightness and belonging he'd known with Ali. She'd loved the young man who'd been a dreamer and, even if she hadn't said the actual words that afternoon, he knew she loved the man who'd made those dreams into reality.

The kicker was she didn't trust him.

In business, Luke's word was as good as a signed contract. He said what he meant and meant what he said. No one had questioned that in a good decade. Yet Ali didn't believe him when he told her he could live anywhere as long as it meant they would be together. She didn't trust him to stick around this time.

Of course, he'd botched it all badly by bringing her to New York and making it seem as if it were the city that had changed his life when, in fact, she had.

Tossing the remains of his drink down the sink, he went in search of his cell phone. If she needed proof that he was a man of his word, then by God, he would give it to her.

When Ali returned to Trillium she threw herself into her duties at the resort. Work had always been her anchor. Keeping busy was what had helped her through heartache the last time. This time, however, no matter how many hours she logged behind her desk at Saybrook's, and no matter how bone-tired she was when she finally collapsed into bed at night, she thought of Luke.

I love you.

Had she made a mistake by leaving? Luke seemed to be trying to convince her she had. He'd left a couple of messages on her answering machine and had fired off half a dozen e-mails. She hadn't responded to any of them, though. Now, a week after her return, she walked into her office after lunch to find two dozen red roses spilling out of a vase on the desk. Audra walked in just behind her, a squirming puppy cuddled in her arms. She settled into a chair as Ali reached for the card tucked amid the blooms. Her sister had been making noises about starting a family. Apparently she'd decided to start with a pet and work her way up to children.

"Luke sent you something," Audra said.

Ali's gaze flicked over the roses. She'd never been a fan of the flower. They were too pricey and they faded too quickly. Now carnations, those lasted.

"Apparently he doesn't remember what I like," she murmured, opening the envelope. The name signed on the card, however, was not Luke's.

"They're from Bradley," she said on a frown.

"Figures," Audra snorted. "He doesn't know you very well, does he? You're too practical for roses."

"He's nice," Ali said defensively, even though guilt

nipped her since she hadn't returned his last two phone calls, either.

"Look." Audra blew out a deep breath as she tried to keep the bundle of brown and white fur from escaping her lap. "I've held my tongue for weeks on this, waiting for you to figure it out on your own, but I can't keep quiet any longer. He's not nice, Ali."

"I know Luke said Bradley was the one making inquiries about the property we purchased. He even claimed Bradley had bid on Saybrook's when it was first put on the market, but we own the resort and the extra acreage now, Audra, and he's *still* interested in seeing me." Ali was feeling raw emotionally, which was perhaps why she added, "Apparently, he *likes* me. Maybe he even *loves* me."

Audra worried her lip for a moment before saying quietly, "If those really are his feelings, Ali, ask yourself why he's hit on me half a dozen times in the past few months."

"What?" she asked, not even realizing she'd crumpled the card in her fist.

"I know you might not want to believe me—"

But Ali stopped her. "I believe you, Aud. We're well past that point. Which is why I have to ask, why didn't you say anything before now?"

Audra stroked the puppy. Her voice was barely above a whisper when she replied, "I couldn't bring myself to do it. You and I had finally settled our differences, a fact

Bradley knew and exploited. I kept hoping you'd see his true colors."

"Does Seth know?"

Audra snorted out a laugh then and glanced up. "The man's alive, what do you think?"

"I guess not. But he doesn't like Bradley."

"No. Seth caught him ogling me one time and that was enough to put his back up. Dane's no fan, either, for the same reason."

"Why is it I feel like I'm always the last to know everything around here?" Ali sighed.

The puppy finally managed to scoot off Audra's lap. It loped around the room on its oversize paws, sniffing the various corners before finally squatting at Ali's feet.

"Your dog just peed on my carpet," she spluttered, incredulous. "You're going to clean that up."

"Sorry, Alice. But that's not my dog." Audra stood and scooped up the puppy. Dumping the wriggling bundle of fur into Ali's arms, she said, "*This* is what Luke sent you. He said to tell you it doesn't have a pedigree, but it does have loads of potential. He also said to tell you that it will love you unconditionally and follow you wherever you go."

"I don't want a dog," she protested sternly, even as her heart melted a little.

"It needs a home, Ali." Audra turned to leave, but then she stopped at the door. "So does Luke."

* * *

Ali named the dog Harley, even though she didn't intend to keep him. But every time she tried to pack him up and take him to the pound, the sight of his big brown eyes and clumsy oversized paws stopped her. *He'll love you unconditionally,* Luke had claimed. *He'll follow you wherever you go.* Something about that seemed so appealing. And so the second day she had him, Ali invested in a thirty-pound bag of puppy chow, a blue leash and collar and one of those plush canine beds, which she tucked into the corner of her room. Not that the bed's location mattered much to Harley. He whined and carried on that night until she scooped him up and settled him beside her on the mattress.

Ali had to admit, the dog was a good judge of people. When Bradley stopped by to see her later in the week, Harley barked copiously, right after which he nipped off one of the tassels from the man's expensive leather loafers.

Their meeting had started off shaky considering what Ali had discovered, but it had gone downhill rapidly after Harley's disappearing tassel trick. Not only had the guy had the nerve to make some disparaging comments about Audra's character, when confronted with Ali's suspicions about his interest in developing on Trillium, he'd finally come right out and admitted that most of Ali's appeal had been her assets. And he'd meant that physically. No double entendres to sooth her wounded ego. Her heart, of course, had not suffered at all in the exchange.

After he'd gone, she sat on her deck as the sun melted

into Lake Michigan, Harley dozing contentedly in her lap, and questioned her judgment when it came to men. A mocking voice—one that sounded suspiciously like Audra's—kept reminding Ali that she'd believed what she'd wanted to believe because of her own pigheadedness.

Did that apply to Luke as well?

Ali had told him to stay away from Trillium and he had done so for nearly two weeks now. Damn the man for *finally* doing exactly what she asked.

The sound of splintering wood and shattering glass had Ali spearing up in bed the following morning.

Pushing the hair out of her eyes, she peered at the clock: 6:00 a.m. Her first coherent thought was that surely the world would wait until she'd had her first cup of coffee before it came to an end.

Harley whimpered beside her and she reached over to stroke his head. "It's okay, boy. Nothing to be afraid of."

She was just swinging her legs over the side of the bed when she heard the crash again. It was a cloudy morning, rain threatening to accompany the brisk wind that had the curtains whipping back from her open windows. All she could think was that a couple of the big white pines edging the property line had finally tumbled over onto Luke's grandmother's cottage. Despite their vast size, their root systems were notoriously shallow.

She pulled on a pair of shorts and a T-shirt, which

she realized was inside out as she hopped down the steps of the deck, her feet not quite inside the pair of canvas sneakers she'd found by the sliding glass door. Harley hurried after her as she rushed along the beach, where the waves churned white and angry at the shore. When she cleared the trees, though, she stood stock-still, urgency giving way to utter shock.

Trees had not crashed into Luke's grandmother's home. A wrecking ball had. And the person at the controls of the crane wielding that ball was none other than Luke Banning.

"Good morning!" he called out cheerfully.

"What in the hell are you doing?" she shouted from the beach.

Clearly he'd lost his mind. Yet he looked perfectly sane. Perfectly…happy as the place where he'd spent a good deal of his boyhood lay in ruins.

"Taking a page out of Audra's book, I guess. I've decided to start fresh."

She didn't have a clue what the man was talking about.

"By taking a wrecking ball to Elsie's cottage?"

"Tom Whitey said the place needed so much work to restore its structural integrity that it almost wouldn't be worth it. Besides, it's my cottage," he said, his grin receding. "It has been for eleven years. You're the one who said we needed to accept the past and then move on. Well, I finally am. Sometimes you have to tear things down to do that."

Her heart sank. "So, you're dividing the property and selling it then?"

"Nope. I'm building. Rebuilding, actually." He hopped off the crane and jogged down the steps that led to the beach, meeting her on the shore. Harley barked and Luke knelt down to rub the puppy's belly. "I see that you kept him."

She shrugged. "I couldn't bring myself to take him to the pound. Thank you, by the way."

"You're welcome." He squinted up at her. "See any potential here yet?" he asked softly.

The puppy got up and began chasing his tail in circles. After a moment, Harley fell over, dizzy but victorious, with the appendage clamped between his teeth.

Ali couldn't help but laugh. "I'm not sure about potential, but he has the unconditional love part sewn up, and he does follow me everywhere."

Luke straightened and tucked a handful of her hair behind her ear. "Told you so," was all he said, and Ali got the feeling he was talking about more than the dog.

"I n-named him Harley, by the way. I figured it suited his rebel spirit." She made a face. "He peed on the carpet in my office the first day I had him."

"I'm glad you were able to overlook his faults."

"We all have them," she said on a shrug. "He also chewed the tassel off one of Bradley's shoes."

"I owe him a juicy bone for that," Luke said, his expression turning tight. "So, how is Bradley?"

"Oh, I'm sure he's fine. You know alley cats, they always manage to land on their feet."

One side of Luke's mouth crooked up. "An alley cat, huh?"

She rolled her eyes on an exasperated sigh. "You were right about him. Satisfied? It turned out he was only interested in my assets and not, well, my *assets,* even though he apparently tried to grope Audra's a time or two."

Luke swore. "Want me to beat him up for you?"

"No. Dane and Seth have already offered, but Bradley's the type to sue. No sense letting him get a foot in the door at Saybrook's over my bruised ego."

"I'm sorry, Ali." One side of his mouth crooked up, though. "Not sorry that he's out of the picture, of course, just sorry that he disappointed you."

She waved off his apology. "I can survive disappointment."

They regarded one another in silence as the wind howled and the gulls screamed overhead. Then he said, "Want to see the plans for the new house?"

"You're really going to build a vacation home on Trillium?"

Luke just shook his head as he walked up the steps ahead of her. "For a smart woman, Alice, you're pretty slow. I told you I was relocating."

"But you belong in New York, Luke. You love it there."

He stopped walking and turned, his face a study in sincerity. "I *enjoy* New York. I *love* you. And I've learned something during the past several weeks, something I've apparently done a poor job of convincing you of."

"What's that?"

"I left here to make something of myself because I didn't figure I was good enough for you, but I'm good enough now."

"Oh, Luke. You were good enough before. I never needed convincing."

"Maybe not, but I did. At the time, I needed to leave. I need to come back now. If you don't believe that today, that's okay. I'm not going anywhere. I'm going to build a house here. A house I plan to turn into a home. And I'm going to wear you down. One day at a time. You know how determined I can be."

"Pigheaded," she corrected. But without malice. How could she be angry when he was looking at her like that?

"I don't belong in New York, Ali. I belong wherever you are. You're my home."

He meant it. She could see that now. Because her chin had begun to quiver, she raised it. "Forever?"

One side of his mouth quirked into a smile. "Is that a proposal, Alice?"

Her heart thumped against her ribs. "It might be. Answer the question."

"Forever."

Ali was smiling as Luke closed the distance between

them. And she was crying when she opened her once shattered heart as wide as the arms that were reaching for him.

"I love you, Ali," he said fiercely.

"I love you, too." Just before their mouths met, she whispered, "Welcome home."

HARLEQUIN® *Romance*

A family saga begins to unravel
when the doors to the Bella Lucia
Restaurant Empire are opened...

The Brides of Bella Lucia

*A family torn apart by secrets,
reunited by marriage*

AUGUST 2006

Meet Rachel Valentine, in
HAVING THE FRENCHMAN'S BABY
by Rebecca Winters

Find out what happens when a night of passion is followed
by a shocking revelation and an unexpected pregnancy!

SEPTEMBER 2006

The Valentine family saga continues with
THE REBEL PRINCE by Raye Morgan

Page-turning drama…

Exotic, glamorous locations…

Intense emotion and passionate seduction…

Sheikhs, princes and billionaire tycoons…

This summer, may we suggest:

THE SHEIKH'S DISOBEDIENT BRIDE

by Jane Porter

On sale June.

AT THE GREEK TYCOON'S BIDDING

by Cathy Williams

On sale July.

THE ITALIAN MILLIONAIRE'S VIRGIN WIFE

On sale August.

With new titles to choose from every month,
discover a world of romance in our books written
by internationally bestselling authors.

If you enjoyed what you just read,
then we've got an offer you can't resist!

Take 2 bestselling
love stories FREE!
Plus get a FREE surprise gift!

HOTEL MARCHAND

**Four sisters.
A family legacy.
And someone is out to destroy it.**

**A captivating new limited
continuity, launching June 2006**

The most beautiful hotel in New Orleans,
and someone is out to destroy it. But mystery,
danger and some surprising family revelations
and discoveries won't stop the Marchand sisters
from protecting their birthright...
and finding love along the way.

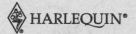
HARLEQUIN®

HARLEQUIN ROMANCE®

Coming Next Month

#3903 A NINE-TO-FIVE AFFAIR Jessica Steele

Emily Lawson is caring for her beloved grandmother, but her gorgeous boss Barden Cunningham doesn't know this—he thinks that she's not taking her work seriously. Things get worse when she drives through snow to deliver a report to Barden and crashes her car. When she's forced to stay with him, Emily realizes that seeing him out of work is quite different from sharing an office!

#3904 HAVING THE FRENCHMAN'S BABY Rebecca Winters

Rachel Valentine is a wine buyer for the Valentine family's exclusive Bella Lucia restaurants and her relationship with winemaker Luc Chartier should be strictly business. Seduced by the vineyards and Luc, Rachel falls in love. But their one night of passion is followed by a shocking revelation about Luc's past. Heartbroken, Rachel returns home to find that she is pregnant.

#3905 SAYING YES TO THE BOSS Jackie Braun

Regina Bellini doesn't believe in love at first sight, but then she is forced to work for the one man who makes her heart stand still— Dane Conlan. The storm brewing within her is undeniable, and that could be enough to tempt her into saying yes to her boss, in spite of what—and who—stands between them.

#3906 WIFE AND MOTHER WANTED Nicola Marsh

Brody Elliott is a single dad struggling to bring up his daughter, Molly. Brody is determined to protect his little girl from heartbreak again. So when Molly befriends their pretty new neighbor, Clarissa Lewis, Brody is wary. Clarissa instantly bonds with Molly. If only Brody was willing to let go of his past and give in to their attraction, maybe Clarissa could be his, too.

HRCNM0706